MISTRESS OF SEABROOK

When her exiled father dies, Victoria comes to England from her native America to clear his name, but things go wrong from the outset. She meets her unscrupulous uncle, Landers Radbourne, and his hateful family, and begins to realise what an impossible task she has taken on. Greed and jealousy lead to a murderous climax, putting Victoria's very life in jeopardy . . .

PHYLLIS MALLETT

◆

MISTRESS OF SEABROOK

Complete and Unabridged

LINFORD
Leicester

First published in Great Britain in 1987

First Linford Edition
published 2014

A catalogue record for this book is available
from the British Library.

ISBN 978–1–4448–1828–4

Published by
F. A. Thorpe (Publishing)
Anstey, Leicestershire

Set by Words & Graphics Ltd.
Anstey, Leicestershire
Printed and bound in Great Britain by
T. J. International Ltd., Padstow, Cornwall

This book is printed on acid-free paper

1

Towards the end of November 1882 a coach rattled and bounced along the rutted road to Tregston in Cornwall. The sky was like granite. Rain gusted down incessantly, powered by a stiff, cold breeze. Although it was barely two in the afternoon the darkening sky suggested an untimely twilight. The driver, muffled in cloak, cape and blankets, hunched his shoulders against the hostile elements. His feet were cold, his eyes red-rimmed, his whole body wracked with discomfort as he cracked his whip repeatedly urging on the straining horses. Already he was thinking of the warmth and refreshment that would be his when they reached the little town. The wheels of the vehicle grated and creaked, and the carriage shook under the blasts of wind which came out of the east from across the stormy sea where the long rollers of the Channel seethed angrily.

The interior of the coach was clammy and dank, the windows tightly closed to retain what little warmth emanated from the occupant huddled on the rear seat under several rugs. Victoria Radbourne was wedged into a corner, holding onto a leather strap with a gloved hand. She was wearing a heavy travelling cloak and bonnet, but she still felt the damp, freezing atmosphere seeping through her protective clothing.

The poor light of the afternoon pressed against the mud-stained windows, and Victoria, her gaze unfocused beyond the glass, was wondering when the long journey would finally come to an end. She was thousands of miles from home, and although her father's family had lived in England for generations, she could not accept it as anything but alien.

She was feeling tired and dispirited, and yet the promise that her father, Durwood Radbourne, had extracted from her upon his deathbed in America kept her from succumbing to despair. Mud and rain combined with the ceaseless wind to weary her and the winter in England was scarcely conducive to travel but the English lawyer who'd written to her had urged her to make the trip to Seabrook Manor without delay.

Victoria's father had stressed the problems she would encounter there. She was aware that unknown difficulties awaited her arrival at Seabrook Manor. Her Uncle Landers Radbourne was completely unscrupulous and had to be thwarted in his desire to claim the Radbourne estate for himself. She was the rightful heir and the injustice inflicted on her father many years before had spurred her on, but the real urgency in her trip to England was the fact that Fenton Radbourne, her grandfather, was old and nearing death.

The coach lurched suddenly and she turned her head quickly to gaze through the window on her right. Mud splashed against the glass, mingling with the streaming rain, but Victoria caught a glimpse of another carriage. For a brief moment the vehicles drew level. Her driver's voice, raised in angry protest, reached her ears. The next moment the big, churning wheels of the two vehicles locked on impact.

Victoria felt the shock of the collision and horror filled her for it seemed that the coach would overturn. The grating wheels left the ruts and the vehicle tilted alarmingly as it was forced off the road. The nearside wheels mounted a bank and Victoria was flung heavily along the dank leather seat.

The vehicle careered to an impossible angle, as she clung desperately to a handhold. An ominous splintering noise cut through the heavy atmosphere. Then the coach toppled over on its side, glass shattering, and Victoria was thrown violently from her seat. As the coach slithered to a halt, her right hand was caught in the looped strap she had been gripping, and for a few, heart-constricting moments she supported herself with one slim arm.

There was no sound from the driver, but, as Victoria began to move gingerly she heard footsteps thudding across the treacherous road and raised voices. The loudest was filled with anger and outraged authority.

'Damn it, Tench, when I told you to make for home as quickly as possible I didn't intend for you to drive every other carriage off the road. Attend to that horse! Get your pistol and shoot it! I'll look for the coachman and see if there are any passengers.'

'I'm sorry, Master Thomas. But if Mr Irvine is dying of a stroke then you need to get home in haste.'

'But not at the expense of other lives, you fool! Look to that horse now.'

Victoria began to struggle to her feet, dazed and shocked, in the gloomy interior of the crippled vehicle. The coach shuddered as someone outside began to clamber upon it. The next instant the upper door was dragged open and the head and shoulders of a man appeared.

'By Heavens! There is a passenger!' he exclaimed. 'If she has suffered harm you'll pay dearly for your recklessness, Tench.'

'I appear to be none the worse for this mishap,' Victoria said tremulously.

'Give me your hands and I'll lift you clear,' the man commanded. He was shapeless in a black cloak and a beaver hat.

Victoria held up her hands obediently, felt them grasped by stronger hands, and was lifted out of the carriage. Rain stung her face as she was set down upon the muddy road, and she glanced around, immediately averting her gaze from the sight of a horse down in the mud at the side of the road. She saw the motionless figure of her own driver stretched out some yards behind the coach. As she picked up her skirts and hurried to his side the report of a pistol shot ripped through the wailing of the wind, and she flinched.

Her heart seemed to miss a beat as she bent over her driver. His face was upturned to the driving rain and he was quite inert. She sensed that he was dead before she reached out a trembling hand to touch him, and when she failed to find any sign of life she arose and looked at her rescuer, who also bent to examine the driver.

'He's dead!' the stranger said. 'You'd better come to my coach.' He took her arm and led her through the mud to where his vehicle had stopped.

'Come in out of the rain.' The stranger grasped her elbow and then almost lifted her into his carriage.

She turned her attention to her rescuer, a tall, strongly built figure whose face was shadowed in the gloom. His noticeably handsome features, although tanned, were pallored by shock. His expression was one of concern. He appeared to be in his middle 20s, and by his speech and bearing was obviously a gentleman of some quality.

'I'm Thomas Walford,' he said, studying her pale face with interest and curiosity. 'May I ask what you were doing in that carriage?'

'Travelling to Tregston.' Victoria sat down suddenly, her legs trembling as reaction gripped her.

'That much was obvious even before our carriages collided,' he said gently, trying to fathom her expression, partially obscured by the brim of her hat. Instinctively he admired her erect head and glistening brown eyes. She seemed remarkably self-possessed, only her gloved hands, clenched in her lap betrayed tension.

'Your coach belongs to the lawyer Spilsby. Are you related?'

'No. I am a Radbourne.'

'A Radbourne! But I know the Radbournes very well — one of them, at least.' For a moment there was a rueful note in his voice. 'I have never seen you at Seabrook before, and you have a strange accent which I do not recognise. You must be a very distant member of the family.'

'Very distant,' Victoria agreed. 'I am from America. My father was Durwood Radbourne.'

'Durwood Radbourne!' Walford's surprise was complete. 'I beg of you, please forgive me! I seem to be repeating everything you say. But the Radbourne family is eminent in these parts, and Durwood Radbourne has been a legend for longer than I can remember.'

'I don't doubt that!' A defensive note crept into Victoria's voice. 'Perhaps my arrival will serve to clear my father's name.'

At that moment the coachman approached, and Thomas Walford excused himself and alighted. Victoria could hear muttered conversation between the two, then Walford joined her, his handsome face set in harsh lines.

'Your carriage is not roadworthy. We are only a few miles from Tregston so I shall take you the rest of the way. Tench is transferring your luggage at this moment. My father has suffered a stroke, hence my urgency. We are neighbours of the Radbourne family, living in Briarwood Hall. I apologise for the recklessness of my coachman, but what is done cannot be undone. When we reach town I shall set you down upon the doorstep of the Spilsby household and arrange for someone to attend the trouble here.'

'Thank you.' Victoria tried to relax. Moments later a whip cracked and the vehicle swayed into motion, proceeding at a steadier pace than before. Victoria drew a shuddering breath and felt her erratic pulse steady at last.

It was a bad omen that the death of Spilsby's coachman should herald her arrival, but glancing at Thomas Walford's tense face reminded her that others had heavy burdens.

'I think it would be better to drive you directly to Seabrook instead of passing its gates and going on to Tregston and the lawyer's,' Thomas said presently.

'Oh, but no-one other than Fenton Radbourne and the lawyer know of my existence!' Victoria spoke worriedly. 'It would not do for me to arrive at Seabrook unannounced.'

'What? Landers and his brood have no idea that Durwood had a family?' Thomas demanded, his pale eyes glittering speculatively. 'No wonder Fenton wanted to keep your existence quiet!

'Nevertheless, I feel we ought to get you to the nearest shelter, and Seabrook is just across the river. Fenton is still the master there, although he is feeble and near death, so I've heard. However, you must decide. Shall we drive directly to Seabrook or add another five miles to your journey?'

'Take me to Seabrook,' Victoria decided.

Walford opened the window and called out to the coachman. Rain spattered in, and Victoria shivered as the merciless wind raked them. She drew her cloak more tightly around her slim body. Walford fought to close the window, then smiled reassuringly at her as he sat down opposite upon the jolting seat.

Minutes later the coach rumbled over a bridge, and Victoria glimpsed a dark, swift-flowing river. Then they passed through tall iron gates into an avenue lined on either side with leafless trees whose stark branches interlaced overhead.

'This is Seabrook,' Thomas said. 'Briarwood Hall is six miles to the east.'

'I'm afraid that I've taken you out of your way, and your trip is of the utmost urgency,' Victoria apologised.

'We have my coachman to blame for the delay,' came the quick response. 'He'll have cause to remember this day for many years to come. But look from the window there and you will presently catch your first glimpse of Seabrook Mansion. The Radbournes have lived here for many generations.'

'I am very well acquainted with the history of my family,' Victoria explained as she leaned to the right and peered through the murky coach window. Trees obstructed her view, but presently the avenue curved to the left and a part of the mansion slid suddenly into view. She caught her breath at the sight of cold grey stone and a stark outline rising above the tops of the trees. Despite the fact that her father had often drawn pictures of the mansion, she felt a quiver of anticipation and no little sense of awe as she gazed at the towers, buttresses and turrets presented for her inspection.

The grey sky with its scudding clouds formed an ominous background to the outline of the roof with its many angles and facets of dull slate. Rain showered to obliterate some of the details, and trees partially obscured the lower storey and ground floor of the building, but the mansion was there, just as she had always pictured it. A sigh escaped her, and Thomas Walford's gentle voice cut through her intent thoughts.

'Is it what you expected?'

'I knew what to expect, but was not prepared for the reality of it,' she replied. She shivered as the coach drew up beside a smooth, glistening terrace in front of the mansion. Towering walls, smothered in creepers, seemed to stretch up to the clouds, and several rows of blank windows stared down inscrutably.

Shrugging off a fleeting sense of dread, Victoria alighted quickly, and Walford escorted her to the big black door that opened as they approached, as if someone inside the house had anticipated their arrival, unscheduled as it was.

A thickset man of portly build confronted them. He was getting on in years, with greying sideburns, and his eyes were steady as he regarded them curiously.

'Seldon, isn't it?' Thomas demanded stiffly. 'Let us into the house without delay.'

Victoria was trying to peer past the butler for her first glimpse of the interior of the mansion. The atmosphere was dense and oppressive. Rain spattered about them as they paused at the door, although Thomas kept edging forward, intent upon gaining entrance.

'I don't understand, Mr Walford,' the butler replied, barring the way with his heavy body, one large hand outstretched to hold the door half-closed. 'Who is this young woman and why have you brought her here?'

'This is Miss Victoria Radbourne, the daughter of Durwood Radbourne!'

'Master Durwood's daughter!' Seldon's voice crackled with shock. He narrowed his eyes and peered into Victoria's face. 'The Lord preserve us!' he exclaimed. 'Please follow me.'

Victoria had a glimpse of a great wood-panelled hall shrouded in shadow. A curved wide staircase curved to the upper regions, flanked on either side by a massive balustrade. Suspended from the ceiling, squarely above the foot of the stairs, was a great chandelier of small lamps.

Their footsteps echoed eerily as

Seldon led the way across the polished floor to a door on the right, but before they reached the drawing room a figure appeared from the gloom on the stairs and a harsh voice demanded an explanation for their intrusion.

Seldon paused and turned to face the newcomer, and Victoria gasped in shock when she peered at the man still descending the staircase. For a moment she fancied that her father was not dead but here in the flesh back in the house where he had been born, but this was Landers Radbourne, her uncle.

'It is Mr Thomas Walford with Durwood's daughter!' There was a vague grain of triumph in Seldon's steady tone.

'So you have arrived at last!' Landers Radbourne stepped off the staircase and advanced to confront them, his eyes intent upon Victoria. 'Victoria Radbourne, I believe.'

'You were aware of my existence and intended arrival?' she asked in some surprise.

'Certainly.' Landers smiled. 'Since my father took to his bed I have been handling family matters. We've been expecting you for some time.'

'Then I will take my leave,' Thomas interrupted quickly. He faced Victoria, ignoring the silent Landers, and spoke apologetically. 'Once again I must apologise for the accident on the road. Perhaps you will permit me to call upon you in a few days so that we can be properly introduced?'

'I shall be pleased to see you again,' Victoria replied. 'I do hope you will find your father in better health and I am sorry to be the cause of your delay.'

Landers stepped forward, intent upon cutting the leave-taking short, and Thomas departed with Landers at his back. When he returned there was a smile upon his face and his dark eyes glittered. Slowly he studied the slight figure of the girl who had arrived to claim the estate he coveted for his own.

Victoria arose to face him, sensing a great need for caution. Any man who could cause his own brother to be disgraced and disowned would not easily abandon his plot to own Seabrook. She must remain vigilant. Perhaps her impulsive journey had been foolhardy for there could be no genuine welcome for her here.

2

'You didn't pick the best time of the year for your long journey,' Landers said smoothly, coming across the room to stand before Victoria. He was dressed in a dark brown suit made of rough material, the high, starched collar of his shirt constricted his fleshy neck. 'Perhaps you were ill-advised to leave America when you did. But no doubt you are concerned about your grandfather's health and desired to arrive before his death.'

'Is he in any immediate danger?'

'My father is almost eighty-four years old! He cannot hope to live much longer.' Landers paused and the shadow of a smile touched his lips.

Victoria looked at his high-bridged nose, broad forehead and dark eyes under heavy brows. He could have been her father but for the intangible expression of disdain and cold calculation in the eyes.

'Your father died last year, I understand,' Landers continued. 'I always thought Durwood was delicate in health. It seems hereditary, for at least one member of each generation seems to be a weakling and not worthy of living. I have two sons and a daughter, whom you will meet shortly, and, of the three, my son Benjamin is the least likely to make old bones.

'I have instructed Seldon to have a room prepared for you. Your grandfather wishes to see you as soon as possible, but tomorrow morning will suffice for that meeting, if the old man still breathes come daylight.'

An angry retort rose to Victoria's lips but she stifled it. She would not react to his callous behaviour, however provoked. Clearly he was seeking an opportunity to show her the dislike he harboured for his brother's daughter.

A hand rapped at the door and Landers turned away while Victoria sighed inaudibly in relief at having been spared further ordeal. The door was opened by a maidservant, who smiled as she curtseyed.

'The room is ready now, Master,' she reported, her gaze upon Victoria. She was plump, and her starched apron rustled as she moved. Her face was round, almost featureless with fat, but her brown eyes were alive with curiosity.

'Very well, Daisy.' Landers spoke in a clipped tone. He waved a casual hand towards Victoria. 'Here is Miss Victoria Radbourne, my niece from America. Show her to the room and ensure that she is made comfortable.' He turned to Victoria once more, as the maid bobbed another curtsey. 'I'll see you at dinner, no doubt, and then you will meet the rest of this household. Now you must excuse me. I wish to break the news of your arrival to my father.'

'Thank you — ' Victoria hesitated for a moment, then added, 'Uncle.'

Landers paused. His features were

inscrutable in the afternoon twilight that entered at the tall windows.

'I think we can dispense with that kind of formality,' he said harshly. 'You are no longer a child. I was christened Landers, and would prefer you to use that name when addressing me.'

He departed then, and Victoria clenched her hands. Daisy held open the door and Victoria followed her into the hall. Large portraits of previous generations of Radbournes peered down at her as she ascended the wide staircase and walked along a gallery to an opened door which led into a large bedroom.

The room was cosy, with a log fire blazing fiercely in the grate. There was a thick red carpet on the floor and heavy brocade curtains at the window. Shrouds of mist were swirling outside the panes, and Victoria suppressed an involuntary shudder as she turned her back to the depressing sight.

'You must be weary after your long journey, Miss, and shocked after the accident,' Daisy said. 'There is tea, and your luggage has been brought up.'

Victoria looked around critically, and found the room tastefully furnished. The furniture was of highly polished walnut which gleamed in the firelight, and the four-poster bed was covered with a fringed white counterpane. Daisy crossed to the window and peered out before closing the curtains. The leaping flames of the log fire filled the room with living shadows, but Daisy lit a lamp and turned the wick high to dispel the gloom. She smiled reassuringly at Victoria.

'That's better! This time of the year, the afternoons are so short. I've been instructed to stay with you if my company is desired. Although it is your family home, you may feel strange and unsettled.'

'Thank you, Daisy.' Victoria suddenly felt the strain under which she had been labouring since the accident. She crossed the room, removing her bonnet and cape, and sank down upon the foot of the bed with a weary sigh.

'Are you all right, Miss?' Daisy approached quickly, her homely face showing concern. 'You weren't hurt in that accident, were you?'

'I'm all right, thank you. I'm shaken, that's all.'

'A nice cup of tea will do you good,' Daisy said confidently, moving to a tray which had been placed on a small, inlaid table. 'Then I'll unpack your luggage. Are you staying here long, Miss?'

'As far as I know, I am here for good.' Victoria was watching the maid as she spoke and saw a shadow cross the girl's face.

'If there's anything you don't like about the room, Miss Maitland's the housekeeper, and she'll be on your side, Miss.' Daisy smiled encouragingly as she poured tea from a silver teapot into a china cup.

'On my side?' Victoria queried, and saw the maid's expression change again.

'I do run on a bit,' the girl admitted, flushing a little. 'I hope you'll forgive me, Miss. But Seldon says I've never got my feet on the ground and precious little in my head.' She brought the cup of tea to Victoria, smiling in a friendly fashion.

'I'll need my dresses, Daisy, if I'm to meet Landers' family at dinner. Perhaps you'll start by unpacking the large trunk.'

'Certainly, Miss!' Daisy was anxious to please.

'And tell me about Landers' family.' Victoria produced her luggage keys.

'I daren't talk about them, Miss!' Daisy retorted quickly, almost snatching the keys from Victoria and turning to the trunks. 'It'd be more than my job is worth.'

'I don't want to hear gossip about them!' Victoria spoke sharply. 'I just want to know who they are.'

'Oh, Miss! I'm sorry!' Daisy flushed deeply. She bent over the trunks, trying the keys in the locks while she continued. 'You've met Master Landers. His eldest son is Ashley. He's about thirty, and his wife is Elizabeth. Then there's Marina, the daughter. She'd be about your age — twenty-five.'

'I'm twenty-four,' Victoria said.

'Benjamin is the youngest son. He's twenty-one.' Daisy raised the lid of the largest trunk. 'He works on the estate. He does more than the rest of them put together. But he's hard to please, and sometimes it isn't safe for a girl to walk about the house alone, if you know what I mean. I'm not being disrespectful, Miss. Benjamin had an accident when he was young and it affected his head. But perhaps it would be better if you wait until dinner and meet them personally. Then you'll see what I mean.'

Victoria nodded, and sat drinking her tea, trying to relax. But she was tired, and the untimely accident had sapped her strength. She looked around the room, her thoughts moving sluggishly, while Daisy unpacked the luggage and put the clothes away in the wardrobe.

A sigh escaped her as she considered her uncle. He was bland, correct in his attitude, but his eyes betrayed him. She knew by her father's words that Landers was unscrupulous, and despair filled her as she considered the future.

'Now you've finished your tea I'll have hot water brought up for a bath. That will do you good, Miss.' Daisy was cheerful again, and Victoria nodded as she tried to find peace of mind. Perhaps she would find something of him in this house to guide and strengthen her faltering spirit.

Despite her tiredness, Victoria discovered that a hot bath did much to dispel her weakness and shock. She dressed for dinner in a simple black gown that enhanced her elegant figure. Daisy fluttered around her, only too happy to brush and tend Victoria's shoulder-length black hair.

When she was ready, Victoria asked Daisy to conduct her to the drawing room. Her heart was beating fast when Daisy ushered her in and closed the door behind her, leaving Victoria alone upon the threshold of the large room.

In the far corner four figures were grouped around a blazing log fire. Landers was not present, Victoria realised as she approached the group. There were two men and two women, silent and watchful. The air crackled with tension. Still no-one spoke.

The two women, both in their 20s, were seated in deep, upholstered chairs, one either side of the fire. The heavier of the two men was standing on the left, and he turned abruptly to a side table and poured himself a drink into a crystal goblet from a silver decanter. The younger man was sprawled carelessly upon a couch, an impudent grin on his face. Victoria's breath caught in her throat. She could expect no welcome here.

Then Landers' harsh voice rang out from the doorway, shattering the silence.

'Ah!' he said in a mock-jovial tone. 'So you are getting acquainted with my family! I hope you're all going to be friendly. We may have to spend considerable time in one another's company before this winter is over. Let me make the introductions. We have some minutes before dinner. Pour drinks for everyone, Ashley . . . '

3

Barely concealing his irritation Ashley returned to the side table, and poured wine into crystal goblets from the silver decanter. When everyone had a glass of the ruby liquid Landers moved to the centre of the floor.

'Let me introduce you, Victoria.' He motioned towards the glowering Ashley. 'My eldest son, Ashley. Thirty years old and a great credit to me.' His expression hardened as he pointed to the older of the two women. 'That's Elizabeth, Ashley's wife.'

'Hello,' Victoria greeted, looking intently at the woman, whose simple blue gown enhanced her slender figure. She had long black hair that was shining in the firelight, and skin as pale as alabaster. Her eyes were dark, but her attractive features were marred by petulance. She waved the hand holding her wine glass, almost spilling its contents over the wide arm of the chair.

'So you've finally arrived,' she remarked in a waspish tone. 'I hope you'll find the place more entertaining than I do!'

'That's enough,' Ashley rebuked, his heavy face showing anger.

'Refill my glass,' Elizabeth commanded, holding it out to her glowering husband.

'Fill it yourself,' he snapped ungallantly.

'My daughter Marina,' Landers continued smoothly.

After being snubbed by Elizabeth, Victoria was not so keen to greet her cousin, but the girl, typical of the Radbourne family, with strong features, dark hair and brown eyes, leaned forward in her seat and actually smiled. She was wearing a dark brown dress that seemed shabby, and her hair looked windswept.

'So you're Victoria,' she commented thoughtfully. 'Of course Uncle Durwood was the black sheep of the family, as everyone knows.'

31

'I'm surprised you had the nerve to come over here,' Ashley said in a grating voice.

'There's no need for that kind of talk within the family circle,' Landers intervened, his expression unsmiling, the mask of affability gone. 'Hold your tongue, Ashley. You show yourself for the clod you are.' He glanced at his younger son. 'Benjamin, behave or you'll be forced to eat with the servants.'

'Perhaps I'd be better off in their company,' Benjamin retorted. 'At least we have something in common; we work for our living.' He cast a disdainful look at his brother, but Ashley turned away to the side table, refilling his glass yet again.

Victoria caught her breath. She was appalled by their behaviour, but fought down her dismay. So this was how her father had been treated at Seabrook!

'Does your family always behave like this or have you something special going on for my benefit?' she demanded.

Landers smiled. 'I admire your spirit,' he commented.

Victoria continued determinedly. 'I will tell you this much. I am here at the invitation of my grandfather, and you had better understand from the outset that I have no intention of being bullied.'

'I agree with you,' Landers smiled. 'I didn't organise this, if that is what you think. My family no doubt fear for their future. They have been brought up on this estate secure in the knowledge that one day I would inherit. It is only natural that you should be considered an outsider, and possibly an enemy.'

The door was opened before Victoria could reply and Seldon announced that dinner was ready.

'Thank you, Seldon.' Landers turned to Victoria. 'I'll escort you.'

'I doubt if they do things like this over in America,' Ashley said with a chuckle as Victoria took Lander's arm. 'Don't they live in log cabins and such?'

'Whatever I lived in,' Victoria retorted,

33

'at least I was taught manners,'

'No doubt you were influenced by your father, but what he told you concerning his youth here is not necessarily correct,' Landers rebuked.

They entered the dining room and Victoria was shown to a seat. The meal was not a particularly pleasant one for her, although the surroundings were exquisite. She listened to her cousins talking casually, endeavouring to learn something about them, but her efforts to make conversation were ignored. She remained outside their circle, and even Landers made it obvious that she was an unwelcome intruder.

After eating, Victoria fought down the impulse to leave abruptly. She would not give Landers the satisfaction of seeing her beaten.

'This has been quite an experience,' she told him quietly, and silence fell around the table at her words. Elizabeth was lounging tipsily with her left elbow propped on the table. Marina, lips compressed, was in the act of rising from the table, but she paused and looked at Victoria with a calculating gaze.

'My father did go to great lengths to explain about you, Landers,' Victoria continued, 'and I must confess that sometimes I found it difficult to believe him. But I know now he didn't exaggerate.'

'I know you are biased against me,' Landers said with a sickly smile. 'Your loyalty to your father does you credit, but it has blinded you to the truth of what happened in the past. However, since we must live together in this house I suggest we try to do it amicably.'

'Certainly, if your family will behave like civilised people! Now, if you would excuse me, I'll go to my room. I'm very tired.'

Marina approached the doorway from the opposite end of the table. Trembling with suppressed anger, Victoria swept into the hall ahead of her. During her long voyage she had often visualised her arrival at the ancestral home, but never in her wildest thoughts had she imagined such an inhospitable reception.

'Just a minute,' Marina called as Victoria started to ascend the stairs. 'I want to put you straight on one or two things.'

Victoria paused and turned, fighting for composure. 'If you have anything unfriendly to say then forget it,' she said defensively. 'I'll tolerate no more insults from your family tonight.'

'I'm not concerned about them,' Marina retorted, tossing her head as they ascended the staircase side by side. 'We merely tolerate each other. I have nothing in common with any of them. My father is obsessed with the estate. He has planned to be the master here for longer than I can remember, and he knows no other topic of conversation. My brother Ashley is a foul creature, as intent as Father upon getting his hands on Seabrook in his turn, and he has soured Elizabeth. As for Benjamin, he slaves away on the estate as if it already belongs to him. So don't talk to me about my family. I wish I could disown them as your father was disowned years ago.'

Victoria wondered if Marina's confession was an overture of friendship. But Marina's expression was cold and selfish.

'There's only one thing I want to get straight with you. Stay away from Thomas Walford. I heard that he met you on the road. But Thomas is mine! He is going to marry me! I won't tolerate competition. As long as you understand that we won't be enemies.'

'I can assure you that I have no designs on Mr Walford or anyone else,' Victoria said sharply, frowning.

'That's all right then.' Marina paused at the top of the stairs. Her untidy hair seemed to bristle as she stared at Victoria. 'But I don't envy you,' she said with a grin. 'Are you planning to stay long?'

'As far as I know I'm here for good.'

Victoria stifled a wave of emotion. 'When my father died last year I was left completely alone, and there's nothing for me back there in America. My father told me so much about England, and Seabrook in particular, that when Grandfather contacted me I was willing to leave and come here.'

'So you're over for good, are you?' Marina chuckled. 'Just wait until I tell my father that! He's hoping that you'll go back to where you came from after about six weeks.' She turned on her heel and walked off along the corridor, leaving Victoria to stare after her, and the door of her room slammed with a dull thud which echoed in Victoria's heart like a knell of doom.

Going on to her room, Victoria sat down on the foot of the bed, her spirits sinking to their lowest ebb. At that moment she wished that her father had not burdened her with the promise she'd made just before he died. But no matter what Landers said or did, she would see that justice prevailed.

Going to bed, Victoria was unable to sleep. When she thought over what had occurred during the long, cold day, she had to fight back her tears. Her thoughts went to Landers and his brood. If they hoped to drive her away with their bad manners and rank unfriendliness then they would not succeed.

Overwrought, Victoria lay straining her eyes and ears in the darkness, nervous of the shadows, listening to the creaking sounds of the old house. Then her door rattled! She shrank down nervously, lips compressed as she stared across the room. Was it the wind? She imagined someone on the other side of her door, listening intently for her first scream. She refused to be intimidated, the door was locked and barred; she was secure for the moment. With a final, defiant rattle, the door was silent.

Time crawled by, and Victoria fancied that she would never be able to sleep again, but eventually she drifted into uneasy slumber, to awaken with a start when Daisy knocked at the door next morning. Slipping out of bed, she ran across and unlocked the door, then darted back into bed as Daisy entered, bringing morning tea.

'I hope you slept well, Miss,' the girl greeted.

'I did,' Victoria replied, and watched Daisy busying herself at the fire, reviving it and making it blaze brightly. Glancing around the room, she thought of her fears in the night, and was glad that the daylight seemed to bring a reassuring brightness.

Daisy departed to return shortly with two copper cans of hot water with which to fill the washstand basin, and Victoria moved the screen to one side in order to feel the benefit of the fire while attending to her toilette. Dressed, she descended to the hall, and Seldon appeared and showed her into the breakfast room.

She was relieved to find only Landers at the big table, and he pushed himself to his feet when he looked up and saw her, nodding bleakly. 'Good morning,' he said formally. 'You're to see your grandfather later this morning. He's been asking about you.'

Victoria was relieved that none of her cousins was present, and Landers must have read something in her expression because he smiled as he glanced around at the empty places.

'Don't worry. You won't see any of my brood down here at this time of day. If Marina is up then she'll be out on that black stallion of hers, galloping about the countryside like a mad-woman. Benjamin would have eaten in the kitchen before going out to supervise the running of the estate, although we have a perfectly capable manager. But Ashley and Elizabeth won't put in an appearance much before noon.'

'So it's only at dinner that I'll have to suffer their company,' Victoria responded.

Landers got to his feet and walked to the door without reply, and the door opened just before he reached it to admit a footman. Landers turned to glance at Victoria.

'Be in the hall at ten o'clock,' he said, 'and I'll escort you to your grand-father's room. But you must not tire him out or let him become too excited.'

Victoria nodded, and after he had gone the footman served her with breakfast.

At ten she was waiting in the hall, and Landers eventually appeared from the library, his face solemn. He noted her tense expression.

'This way,' he said curtly, and she followed him in silence up the staircase, lined with sombre portraits of her ancestors. When they reached her grandfather's room, Landers knocked briskly on the door and entered, closely followed by Victoria who looked eagerly at the frail old man propped up in the big four poster bed. He was white-haired, unmistakably a Radbourne, his wrinkled face yellowed like faded parchment. But his eyes were ageless, alert and birdlike.

'Durwood's daughter, Victoria, Father,' Landers called from the doorway, and departed, closing the door upon them.

Victoria could see her own father in the face of this old man, and she struggled with the conflicting emotions that threatened to overwhelm her. Many times in the past she had imagined what she would say to the man who had exiled her father, but now, confronting him, aware of his frailty, bitter words died on her lips and she clenched her hands impotently.

'Durwood's daughter,' Fenton repeated. He lifted a thin hand and beckoned her. 'Come closer. I want to see you clearly and my old eyes are not what they used to be.'

'How are you, Grandfather?' Victoria spoke hesitantly, instinctively looking upon him as another enemy of her father.

'It was very good of you to come all the way from America to satisfy the whim of an old man,' he said softly. 'I am only sorry that your father is not alive to accompany you.'

'You were told that he died last year?'

'I heard. Did he have a good life over there?'

'He lived the best way he knew how without a heart.' She smiled sadly. 'He left that here.'

'Ah! You wound me deeply with your words. If only I could turn back the clock! But, alas, that cannot be.'

'Do you still believe that he was guilty?' she demanded.

'I learned too late that he was innocent.'

'But you never let him know.' Victoria spoke sharply. 'I was with him when he died, Grandfather. It may relieve you to know that he forgave you at the end.'

'He said that?' Fenton lifted a hand to his face and rubbed a knuckle against his cheek — a gesture which reminded Victoria poignantly of her father. 'A great wrong was done,' Fenton continued harshly. 'It is too late to make reparation to your father, but I am trying to set matters right. That is why you are here now. I wish you to regard Seabrook as your home. It will comfort me to know that you are under this roof.'

'I intend to stay,' Victoria said. 'This is my home.'

'Spoken like a true Radbourne!' Fenton's tone wavered slightly, and Victoria, glancing at his wrinkled face and gnarled hands, felt only pity for him. For the first time she realised that he had not willingly exiled her father. He must have suffered from the separation as much as Durwood himself.

Fenton lifted a hand but it fell limply to the bedcovers, and then the old man began to gasp and clench his hands. He slumped back against the pillows, head sagging to one side, frail shoulders inert. Victoria bent over him.

'Grandfather, what's wrong?' she demanded, taking hold of his shoulders and trying to lift him into a more comfortable position. But he was

45

unconscious, breathing heavily, his mouth agape.

She ran to the door and called for Landers, and the next moment he entered the room and went immediately to the bedside. He felt the old man's heart before turning an impassive face towards her.

'I ought to have known better than to let you in,' he snapped. 'If he should die because of your arrival — !' He broke off and hurried from the room.

Victoria looked down silently upon the harshly breathing old man, fighting off her tears. Then Seldon spoke from the doorway and she turned to face him.

'I heard what Master Landers said,' the butler told her. 'I warn you here and now that he intends to inherit this estate. I may be speaking out of turn, but I knew your father very well and always believed in his innocence. I would not want to see ill-fortune befall his daughter here in the very house where he was born.'

'I understand,' Victoria said, returning her gaze to the wrinkled face of her grandfather. 'Perhaps we'd better leave. I assume that Landers is sending for the doctor.'

'Yes, Miss. But very often the doctor never arrives.'

'Do you mean that Landers withholds medical treatment from his father?' She was shocked.

'It's not for me to say, Miss!' Seldon shrugged. 'Now if you would leave I'll take care of the old master. I have nursed him before through these attacks. Perhaps you will be good enough to summon the housekeeper. She knows what medicines I use to keep the life in this old body. I fancy that it is my skills with the herbs that have cheated Landers of what he most desires.'

Victoria nodded as she departed, but she paused in the doorway and looked back at the frail old man in the bed. Her grandfather! She nodded slowly. After all her secret wishes and oft-repeated dreams it had finally come to pass. She was under the roof of the house her father had so sorely missed. But she was not misled into believing that this was the end of her quest. It was only too clear now that her arrival was merely the beginning, and what awaited her she could not even begin to guess . . .

4

As Victoria reached the gallery outside Fenton's room a small wisp of a woman appeared at the top of the staircase, carrying a small leather bag. She was wearing a severe black dress that swept the floor with its hem, and only the toes of her shiny leather shoes protruded from the enfolding material. She was old, her face lined with the experiences of a lifetime in service. Her expression was grim, but it relaxed slightly when she saw Victoria.

'You must be Durwood's daughter,' she greeted. 'I'm Miss Maitland, the housekeeper. Is Seldon in your grandfather's room?' She paused until Victoria nodded, then continued. 'Just let me give him this bag then I will talk to you. Don't worry too much about all this. It will take more than the shock of seeing you to put Fenton

Radbourne into his grave.'

Victoria drew a quivering breath as the old lady entered the room, and waited until she reappeared. Miss Maitland smiled in friendly fashion, a homely little woman with neat white hair and piercing brown eyes.

'Let us leave Seldon to his skills,' she suggested. 'Come down to my room and tell me all about your life in America. I want to hear about your father. It was a tragedy that he ever had to leave Seabrook. If there was any justice in the world things would have been different.'

Landers appeared at the top of the stairs, but Miss Maitland linked her arm through Victoria's and gently tugged her away from the bedroom door.

'We'll use the back stairs. I must say that you resemble the Radbourne family. What was your mother like?'

'Miss Maitland!' Landers' voice thundered along the gallery, and Victoria turned angrily as he approached.

'Have you no consideration for Grandfather?' she demanded. 'He may be dying.'

'If he is then it's because of your arrival,' Landers retorted.

'No.' Victoria shook her head emphatically. 'It will be the result of something that you started many years ago.'

'I feel you have a point there,' Miss Maitland interposed in a mild tone. 'You called me, Master Landers. What do you wish?'

'Hot water. Daisy is off duty now. Perhaps you would be good enough to supervise that new maid and teach her exactly what her duties are.'

'You would deny me the pleasure of talking to Durwood's daughter!' Miss Maitland nodded. 'Very well.'

'I'll deny you a great deal more when my father is finally dead,' Landers snapped.

'How?' Victoria demanded angrily. 'You talk as if you would inherit Seabrook.'

Landers clenched his teeth and fury

showed in his features. Miss Maitland chuckled as she let go of Victoria's arm and went off towards the back stairs.

'We shall talk later,' she said over her shoulder, and Victoria nodded, determined to thwart Landers.

'You had better go down to the front of the house,' Landers directed. 'You'll only be in the way up here. Benjamin is waiting to show you around the estate.'

'I wouldn't dream of leaving the house while this crisis hangs over Grandfather,' Victoria retorted.

Landers chuckled harshly. 'Don't take any notice of his condition,' he snapped. 'The old dog has an attack such as this at least once every week.'

Victoria suppressed an angry retort and turned away. Benjamin was waiting in the hall, a grin upon his youthful face. He was dressed in a short, thick riding coat, breeches and riding boots.

'Hello,' he greeted, and there was so much unexpected friendliness in his voice that Victoria was taken aback. 'How is Grandfather?'

'We must wait and see,' she replied, shaking her head.

'It's fine outside at the moment,' he continued, 'and I wondered if you would like to look over the estate before lunch. Can you ride?'

'Yes.' Victoria was indecisive, although the thought of riding appealed to her, and it was obvious that Benjamin was trying hard to be friendly. 'All right.' She glanced at him. 'If you would give me time to change.'

'Certainly. I'll go and pick a quiet mare for you. The stables are at the rear. Come out through the kitchen door and I'll be waiting for you. It will be a pleasure to have someone to show around.'

It was in Victoria's mind to turn down the invitation but Benjamin seemed so eager that she hadn't the heart to snub him. So she nodded and ascended the stairs to her room, where she quickly changed into her riding outfit; a thick divided skirt and black leather jacket with calf-length riding boots. A glance from the window warned her that the weather might become inclement. The leafless branches of the trees were whipping agitatedly in the gusting wind. She donned a thick riding cape and drew gloves upon her slender hands.

Benjamin was waiting in front of the stables, a groom holding their horses. He nodded approval of her attire and motioned to a bay mare. The groom led the animal, equipped with a side saddle, to a mounting block, but Victoria shook her head.

'I've never ridden side saddle,' she protested.

'All ladies ride in this manner, Miss,' the groom said in a shocked tone.

'All English ladies, I assume,' she retorted. 'But I am an American. Please change the saddle.'

Benjamin chuckled as the groom led the bay into the stable, but the saddle was changed and, when the horse emerged once more, Victoria patted it and mounted quickly. Benjamin swung into his saddle and immediately rode off, leaving her to follow, and their hooves clattered on the damp cobblestones.

It was exhilarating to canter along a rutted path away from the overpowering atmosphere of the house, but presently Benjamin slowed his horse to a walk and moved in beside Victoria. The cold wind blew boisterously about them, tweaking Victoria's cloak and tugging at her hair. The day was cold but not unpleasant, and she began to enjoy the outing.

'I'm glad you like riding,' Benjamin commented. 'I find it very lonely here. Ashley is not the outdoors type and Marina is always riding off on her own. I'm displeased with Ashley. He won't do anything constructive on the estate. All he's interested in are his pleasures.'

Victoria listened intently to Benjamin's grumbles, hoping to learn something of the family, but she soon discovered that he was childish in his attitude and petulant in his conversation. He seemed obsessed with Ashley's position in the family, and her opinion of him diminished as they continued.

She began to suspect that he was jealous of the fact that Ashley was the eldest son, and it seemed as if history was repeating itself, for this was how Landers had begun with Durwood.

'It will be a disaster if Ashley ever gains control of the estate,' Benjamin said angrily, repeating himself yet again. 'He's a wastrel. The estate would go to ruin in no time. But I could manage everything perfectly. I would make it prosper.'

'I'm sure you would,' Victoria answered, sensing that she ought to humour him.

The low clouds scudding overhead suddenly began to emit droplets of rain, and Benjamin glanced around before pointing to a dilapidated mansion situated to their left. Victoria glanced skywards and saw that they were in for a heavy downpour.

By the time they had cantered across overgrown flower beds towards the ruined house the rain was sheeting down, and Benjamin ducked his head and rode straight through the gaping doorway. Victoria dismounted and led her horse inside, flinching as a bird flew out over her head. The distant rumbling of thunder growled through the charged atmosphere, and she held her reins tightly as the mare moved uneasily. Benjamin had dismounted in what had been the hall and was tying his reins to a pillar supporting the gallery which encompassed all sides of the hall on the first floor. He came and fetched the mare, tying her beside his own horse.

'I don't think it will last long,' he commented, moving into the doorway to peer out at the lowering sky.

Victoria stifled a shiver as she peered around. The gloomy interior of the house was in ruins, with pieces of stone and other rubble half filling the great hall. The staircase was rotten, with some stairs broken and splintered, and rain splattered down through holes in the gallery and roof.

'What place is this?' she asked, voice echoing.

'This was the original Seabrook Manor. It fell into ruin, so they built the present place, where you are living now.' Benjamin merely glanced at her while speaking, then quickly returned his attention to the outside, bending forward a little as he peered into the misty distance. 'Come and look at this,' he said sharply, and she joined him.

A rider was galloping recklessly through the sweeping curtains of rain, and Victoria saw a big black stallion. She gasped when the rider put the horse at a tall hedge that lay across its path, and her heart seemed to miss a beat as the animal leaped into the air, clearing the barrier with scant inches to spare. The horse stumbled on landing but the rider picked it up with great skill and disappeared into the distance, leaving sullen echoes of pounding hooves to mark its passing.

'Who was that?' she demanded.

'My sister Marina!' Benjamin chuckled harshly as he glanced at her, his right eyelid twitching. One of these days that stallion will kill her, and good riddance! There's an agreement between Seabrook and Briarwood Hall that she and Thomas Walford shall marry one day, but Thomas would be a fool to commit himself to such a madwoman.'

Victoria stared aghast at him, surprised by his intensity. She fancied he was joking, but his expression was deadly serious and she began to feel afraid. He was mentally deranged! He seemed to hate everyone in his family; his only love was the estate itself. What would his reaction be if she inherited Seabrook instead of Landers? She dared not consider.

She moved back from the doorway, attempting to appear casual, and when one of the horses stamped the unexpected sound startled her. Benjamin did not move from the doorway and she forced herself to advance deeper into the musty interior of the house, finally pausing at the foot of the wide staircase. Rain dribbled down from the upper shadows and somewhere close by a small rodent scuttled through the rubble, its furtive movements unnerving her.

The old house creaked and groaned alarmingly, and when she looked up at the gallery surrounding the hall she fancied she saw a movement in the near darkness.

She froze in shock. A heavy beam was teetering on the edge of the gallery above her, see-sawing violently, and, before she could move, it tipped towards her and came crashing down.

Instinctively she sprang towards the doorway, colliding with her horse. The beam missed her by mere inches, its farther end splintering through the bottom of the stairs with a great crash, and as it rebounded towards her the horses took fright and reared, whinnying and pulling at their reins.

Victoria stumbled to one side, avoiding the lashing hooves. She ran to the door to escape choking clouds as Benjamin steadied the horses. 'I told you the old place was haunted,' Benjamin said, patting the horses and grinning as he gazed at her. 'Obviously the ghosts don't like you.'

'It was no ghost who pushed that beam down,' she retorted fearfully. Go up there and look around. I tell you that I saw the beam see-sawing on the edge of the gallery. Someone was making a great effort to push it over, and I heard a noise up there just before it happened.'

'You're overwrought. And I'm not going up there! You can see for yourself that those stairs are not safe. No man could stand on those rotting boards. They wouldn't take his weight.'

Victoria stifled a sigh and moistened her lips. Her pulses were racing, her heart pounding, and she was very scared. But she drew a deep breath and stepped through the doorway into the driving rain.

'Please bring my horse out,' she said

61

firmly. 'I'm going back to the Manor.'

'It's raining too hard for riding,' Benjamin protested. 'Stand just inside the doorway if you're scared of the place.'

'If you don't bring out the horse then I'll start walking.'

'Wait a minute, I'm coming,' Benjamin called, and led the horses out of the ruins.

Victoria stood in the pouring rain, soaked to the skin and the moaning of the chill breeze through the gaping windows and holes in the masonry added to the coldness in her heart. The house might be haunted, she thought, but that beam could not have fallen as it did without human aid.

Hoisting herself into the saddle, she set off at a gallop before Benjamin could mount, and his surprised shout trailed away into the rain as she rode as fast as the mare could run. Then Benjamin came up on her left and reached across to grasp her reins. She struck at his hand, knocking it away, and her teeth were clenched.

'I thought your horse was running away with you,' he rapped.

'I'm perfectly capable of handling any horse,' she retorted. 'I just want to get back to the Manor.'

A sigh of relief escaped her when she finally crossed the path at the rear of the Manor and entered the yard in front of the stable. She dismounted, and noticed that her right boot was half covered with a dark brown stain, like paint. She must have stepped in it back at the ruined house.

Benjamin joined her, taking the reins of the mare. 'Thank you,' she said in a stilted tone.

'So you don't blame me for what happened back at the old house?' he demanded.

'How could it have been your fault?' She turned on her heel and hurried to the kitchen door, aware that he did not follow her.

Going to her room, she changed into a dress and put silk slippers upon her feet. Then she descended the staircase to find Seldon opening the front door to two visitors. The man and a woman moved across the threshold, Seldon said in a hollow voice, 'Mr Thomas Walford and his sister, Miss Amena, wish to be introduced to you.'

Victoria went forward immediately, her expression brightening. Relief filled her, and the coldness that had settled in the pit of her stomach evaporated as her sense of loneliness diminished. She looked at Amena Walford, who threw back her hood and shook shoulder-length golden hair free from its constriction. The girl held out her hand, a smile upon her lovely face. Her blue eyes were bright and pale as a summer sky.

'How very nice to meet you, Victoria,' she said in a friendly tone. 'Thomas has told me a great deal about you, and as we were passing I just had to come and make your acquaintance and invite you to Briarwood Hall.'

'Thank you. I'm very pleased to meet

you. I'll certainly accept your kind invitation.' Her gaze darted to Thomas, and he bowed slightly, a smile upon his lips.

'I trust you have recovered from the shock of our first meet,' he said in a low tone. His eyes were as blue as Amena's. 'It was a tragic business.'

'The coachman who died!' Victoria's voice quivered. 'Did he have a family?'

'Fortunately he did not.' There was regret in Thomas's well modulated tones. 'There will be an inquest, but I hope you will be spared the ordeal of having to attend. My coachman, the reckless fool, will have to answer for the consequences of his actions. But how have you been received here? Are you enjoying Seabrook?'

'It's a beautiful place.' There was enthusiasm in Victoria's tone despite the shudder that passed through her breast as she recalled the closeness of her brush with death.

The front door was thrust open violently, admitting an icy blast of wind, and Victoria frowned as a figure came striding across the threshold. It was Marina. The girl slammed the door with such violence that the chandelier over the foot of the stairs began to swing wildly.

'Well!' Marina declared, dark eyes glittering moodily as she paused opposite Victoria and gazed at the visitors. 'I took the trouble to ride out in bad weather this morning to visit Briarwood, only to learn, when I arrived, that the Walfords were not at home.'

'We were not expecting you, Marina,' Amena reproached.

'Do I need an invitation now to visit a neighbour?' Marina could scarcely control her anger, and Victoria frowned when she realised that the girl's emotion was directed at her. 'I can remember when I was always welcome there.'

'You ought to have sent word of your intention,' Thomas said quietly, blue eyes gleaming with an icy expression.

Victoria watched closely, interested in

Thomas's reaction to Marina, and it appeared that he was slightly embarrassed by the girl's passion. For a moment he seemed at a loss. Amena, however, touched his arm.

'I fear that we have called at an inopportune moment,' she said. 'It must almost be time for lunch. Forgive us, Victoria, for arriving unannounced, but please do come and visit us. I'd love to hear about your life in America, and I'm sure Thomas will be interested in what you can tell him about the natives over there.'

'The Red Indians!' Victoria smiled. 'Would it surprise you to know that I have never seen one in my life?'

'But I'm sure you do have some very interesting stories to tell,' Thomas insisted, 'and we would derive great pleasure from listening.'

'Thank you. As soon as it's convenient I'll make arrangements to call.' Victoria smiled, but then her face sobered. 'I'm sorry, but I haven't asked. Your father! You were hurrying home to see him when the accident occurred. How did you find him?'

'Better than I feared, but still very ill.' There was momentary sadness in Thomas's voice. 'I'm sure Father would have found you very interesting, Miss Radbourne.'

'Please call me Victoria. My friends call me Vicky.'

'I'll remember that,' Marina snapped. She had remained silent during their brief interchange. She motioned to Seldon, who was standing in the background. 'The Walfords are leaving, Seldon. Please open the door for them.'

Victoria was aghast at such bad manners, but Amena smiled and Thomas bowed. Seldon opened the door and the visitors departed. Closing the door, Seldon turned to confront Marina, his seamed face perfectly expressionless, his tone respectful when he spoke.

'Will there be anything else, Miss Marina?' he inquired.

'Yes, go and boil your head!' the girl

snapped, and her brown eyes glittered as she glared at Victoria. 'I warned you about Thomas,' she snapped jealously. 'He's spoken for.'

Victoria remained impassive, and Marina muttered under her breath and turned away, ascending the stairs two at a time in a most unladylike manner. But she paused at the top and glared down at Victoria before hurrying out of sight. Her footsteps echoed along the upper corridor, and then her door slammed heavily.

Victoria sighed as she let her thoughts ripple across the face of the situation. She was unnerved by her horrifying experience in the ruined house, and would have told Thomas about it if Marina hadn't interrupted. She feared now that Landers intended to get rid of her before she had the chance to inherit, and the coldness that filled her breast seemed to paralyse her mind.

Seldon announced that lunch was ready, and Victoria, although she had never felt less like eating, realised that she had to make an effort to appear unperturbed. If Landers became aware that she suspected his intentions then he might be precipitated into far more deliberate action against her. But her nerves were stretched to breaking point and she wondered how much she could take without cracking under the strain.

5

After the ordeal of lunch, Victoria returned to her room, filled with pessimism. She was alone in this big house with not a single friend to rely upon. Perhaps she had been unwise to place herself at the mercy of Landers and his family. They had a great deal to lose, and very few people knew that she was here at Seabrook. If she vanished, it would be simple for Landers to say that she had gone back to America.

The knock on the door interrupted her gloomy thoughts. It was Daisy, announcing that she had a visitor who was waiting in the library. On her way downstairs, Victoria imagined that Thomas had called again and the thought cheered her. But when she entered the library it was to find Seldon standing there, waiting to take the hat and cloak of a very old man who was tall and thin, white-haired, and incredibly frail. But there was a smile upon his lips as he looked up and caught sight of her.

'Mr Millard Spilsby, the lawyer,' Seldon introduced. 'Miss Victoria Radbourne.'

'My dear young lady!' Spilsby exclaimed, his wizened face creasing into deep lines. 'I have long awaited your arrival. It does my heart good to see the daughter of Durwood Radbourne here in the very house he was born.'

'I feel that I know you very well after the letters that passed between us,' Victoria responded, her spirits rising.

'I spared no efforts to find you,' Spilsby said, taking her hands in his. 'It was a bad business that happened on the road when my carriage was bringing you from the dock. But I trust you are settling in here now.' He paused until she had nodded, and then continued, 'I understand that your grandfather has found meeting you over-taxing.'

'I do hope he will recover.' Anxiety

tinged Victoria's voice as they sat down at the table in the centre of the room.

'You resemble your father,' Spilsby observed. 'Of course, I have not seen him for many years. It's a tragedy that he could not know how his father searched for him. But let us get down to business. How have you been received here?'

'I — er — ' Victoria was hesitant, and refused to meet Spilsby's gaze.

'So it has been like that, has it?' he demanded, nodding. 'It is no more than I expected, and if your grandfather had been stronger I would have advised him to take certain steps for your protection. But he has been confined to his bed and Landers himself has taken over the administration of the estate. So what can I do to make your stay here more comfortable? Have they been giving you a hard time of it?'

Victoria was encouraged by his concern, and related all that had befallen her since arriving. Spilsby listened in silence, his lined face setting into deep creases, and when Victoria lapsed into silence he cleared his throat and spoke in a surprisingly strong voice.

'I must speak upon a matter of some delicacy,' he said. 'You must be aware that your father was innocent of the crime for which he was exiled.'

'That's not a matter of some delicacy!' Victoria retorted. 'I have known about it for many years. My father told me often enough to be on my guard when I arrived. But even if I hadn't been forewarned, the poor welcome I received would have convinced me.'

Victoria went on to relate the incident that had occurred at the ruined house, and Spilsby's eyes filled with alarm. He tut-tutted and then shook his head.

'It would be better if you left this house immediately and never set foot in it alone. But I suspect that you would ignore that advice, so I can only suggest you make friends with the Walfords.

They are a fine family.

'I have received an invitation to visit Briarwood, and will do so immediately,' Victoria said.

'I shall visit often to ensure that all is well with you, but now we must discuss the real reason for my call this afternoon. I have been retired from law practice for many years now, except for this particular case. Your grandfather and I have been much more than lawyer and client, and while this business is unsettled I will entrust it to no-one. You must know that when we discovered your existence, Victoria, Landers was disinherited. When Fenton Radbourne dies Seabrook and the entire estate will belong to you.

'And what will become of Landers and his family? I do not wish them to be homeless.'

'There is Thornton Grange, on the edge of the estate. It is customary for the other members of the family to live there when the present master dies and a new owner takes possession. Landers and his family will have to move out of here.'

'I'm relieved to hear that. Had their attitude to me been different I'd have been willing for the whole family to remain at Seabrook. As it is . . . '

'I expect it will not be pleasant for you over the next few weeks,' Spilsby said. 'And Christmas is barely a month away. However you must endure, but be vigilant.'

With these words of advice the lawyer bade her farewell.

To Victoria's relief the days passed uneventfully enough, though at first she could not sleep easily for fear of intruders and during the day, kept company with Daisy or another member of staff. But there were no unpleasant confrontations with her English relatives.

Benjamin began to ignore her after she refused point-blank to go riding with him again, and the household seemed to slip into a mood of anticipation as Fenton's condition remained stable, apparently hovering between life and death.

Then Ashley began to make a nuisance of himself. He often accosted her in lonely passages or entered one of the rooms when she was there, and despite his sullen manner he seemed to be watching her speculatively most of the time. Once he put a hand upon her shoulder, and she recoiled with horror for his strong fingers were covered with thick black hair between, the upper knuckles and on his powerful wrists.

'I think it would be better if we arranged to avoid each other in future,' Victoria told him as she moved away.

'Your life here would be much happier if we became friendly,' he asserted.

'I'm quite resigned to the situation,' she responded. 'I know where I stand now.'

'You think you're going to inherit when Grandfather dies!' Ashley shook his head. 'Don't be too sure.'

Victoria turned and retreated to her room to avoid further discussion, and afterwards took great care to stay out of

Ashley's way. She decided to talk with the housekeeper, for her brief meeting with Miss Maitland had held the promise of friendship.

Leaving her room, she met Seldon in the hall, and called to him. He approached with his deliberate step, and she wondered if he, too, was scared of showing her any friendliness.

'Is there something I can do for you, Miss Victoria?' he asked.

'I'd like to talk with you! I've been here several days now and would like to know how my grandfather is — Landers will not permit me to visit him since he thinks the sight of me will provoke another attack.

'Your grandfather is as well as can be expected. He is confined to his bed, but not physically ill. Old age has laid him low, and, of course, he must have no excitement.' Seldon paused, then began to move away, glancing back at her as he did so. 'Will there be anything more, Miss?'

'Yes.' Victoria became impatient,

sensing his fear. 'I'd like to know a lot of things, and you and Miss Maitland are probably the only people, apart from Landers and Grandfather, who have the answers to my questions. It's obvious that Landers would never tell me the truth, and poor Grandfather is not well enough to talk. That leaves you and Miss Maitland, but she scurries away like a frightened mouse whenever she sees me, and you act as if I'm a plague-carrier. Have you been warned against talking to me?'

'By whom, Miss?' He glanced around the hall furtively, as if afraid that someone was watching him.

'Landers, obviously.' Victoria clenched her hands. 'He has much to hide, I fear. But my father spoke a great deal about you before he died, Seldon. He thought highly of you, and told me that if I ever needed a friend then I could count on you.'

'I think kindly of your father's memory, Miss Victoria,' Seldon replied in a quiet tone, his wrinkled face showing uneasiness. 'But I have been warned against talking to you. I'm not afraid of losing my job, although that has been threatened. Landers is the master here at the moment, and while I'm in the house nothing untoward will happen. You could say that I am looking after your interests from a distance.'

'I see.' Victoria nodded. 'I appreciate that. But I am not at all happy with the situation. There's much going on now, and a great deal that happened in the past, which I ought to know about.'

Seldon glanced around again, and indecision was showing in his smooth features. 'We can't talk here, Miss,' he said at length. 'Why don't you come into the kitchen for a cup of tea? We should be undisturbed there.'

'Lead on,' she said quickly, and he glanced around once more before turning towards the kitchen.

Miss Maitland was seated at the big kitchen table, and started to her feet in surprise when Seldon entered, followed by Victoria.

'Sit down, please, Miss Maitland,' Victoria said firmly. 'I would like you to listen to the questions I am going to ask Seldon, and perhaps you will be able to either bear out what he says or add to anything he tells me.'

The housekeeper glanced at Victoria, saw the determination in her expression, and sighed.

'I'm an old, old woman,' she said slowly. 'There's nothing anyone can do to me now. I've bottled up my grief and injustice for many years. I loved your father as if he were my own, and the sight of Landers in his place has been a thorn in my flesh. Let me make a pot of tea while Seldon answers your questions.'

Victoria heaved a sigh of relief. Seldon pulled forward a chair close to the fire and motioned for Victoria to be seated. He sat opposite, and for a moment studied her with narrowed eyes.

'What really happened all those years ago?' she urged. 'Tell me,' she commanded.

'First, the 'Green Fire' was stolen!'

'Father mentioned that jewel many times,' Victoria gasped, 'but didn't say that it had been stolen.'

'He was accused of stealing it!' Seldon's tone was grim. 'Although he was innocent the family blamed him.'

'There were other incidents.' Seldon shook his head sorrowfully. 'A young woman came knocking at the door one day, claiming that she was pregnant by your father. There were terrible scenes! Your father denied responsibility and when it seemed to have settled down, the final blow came. The girl's brother accosted your father in Tregston, there was a fight, the brother was killed, and your father fled to America, leaving behind a mess that has never really been settled.'

Victoria remained silent for a moment, and Miss Maitland placed a cup of tea before her. The strong brew warmed Victoria, and she stiffened her shoulders and thrust out her chin.

'Did my father ever admit to any of

this?' she demanded.

'He strongly denied everything, but there was evidence against him. The girl insisted, even after he had gone to America, that he was the father of her child.'

'Father told me many times that Landers was responsible for his exile. Why was nothing done about Landers?'

'He covered his tracks too well.' There was a grim note in the butler's voice. 'That woman had a son, and then went missing with the baby. They were never seen again, and it was rumoured that Landers paid her to leave the district.'

'Poor father!' Victoria caught her breath as emotion prickled behind her eyes. 'So this is what I am up against!'

'You must never forget for a moment that Landers is an evil man,' Miss Maitland urged. 'Always be on your guard, my dear.'

'Thank you.' Victoria got to her feet. 'I am thankful that we have had this chat. It clears the air a great deal. I will be careful in future, and now I understand how far Landers will go to get what he wants I won't underestimate him.'

She left the kitchen and returned to her room, shivering as she sensed an evil air of desolation in Seabrook. But she was here to stay, and no-one was going to frighten her away.

Amena Walford called that afternoon, and Victoria was delighted to have the girl's company. They sat in the drawing room, talking incessantly until Amena had to leave.

'You've been here practically a week now,' Amena said finally, 'and we are keen to have you visit us. Seabrook is so dreary compared to Briarwood, and you have to see our place to appreciate the truth of that. Won't you come?'

'Very well.' Victoria nodded. 'I'll look forward to visiting you tomorrow afternoon.'

'Shall we send our carriage for you?'

'Thank you, but I expect the Radbournes have a carriage, and I can see no reason why I shouldn't have the use of it.'

'Then I'll tell Thomas we can expect you at three tomorrow.' Amena's tone was firm, and she prepared to depart before Victoria could change her mind.

Victoria stood in the hall until the girl had departed, and when Seldon closed the front door his usually staid expression was cheerful.

'I'm so pleased the Walfords want to make friends with you, Miss Victoria,' he remarked. 'It's the best thing that could happen.'

'Thank you, Seldon.' Victoria smiled. 'I shall be visiting Briarwood tomorrow afternoon.

The afternoon was already growing dark, and Seldon began to supervise the lighting of the lamps in the hall. The gallery was gloomy, and the sound of the wind howling outside sent a shiver through Victoria. As she reached the top of the stairs she saw a figure moving towards her, and the next moment

Ashley confronted her, grabbing her wrist.

'So it's the Walfords you're getting interested in, hey?' he demanded, his breath reeking of whisky. 'Isn't your own family good enough for you?'

Victoria drew a sharp breath, an angry retort rising to her lips, but the next instant Landers appeared behind Ashley and seized hold of him, spinning him away from her.

'Ashley, if I ever catch you bothering Victoria again I'll throw you out of the house,' Landers snapped, his voice tremoring with rage.

Ashley glared for a moment, then jerked free and started down the stairs without a further glance at Victoria, who was cold inside, her mind filled with panic.

'I have never met a more ill-mannered man than your eldest son,' she gasped. 'He is more often than not under the influence of drink, and goes out of his way to be nasty to me. Is he acting upon your orders, Landers? Do you seek to drive me out of the house by making my life here intolerable?'

'Don't be ridiculous!' Landers turned away. 'I shall have something more to say to Ashley about this, never fear.'

'While we are talking, perhaps you'll tell me if the Radbournes have a carriage available.' Victoria made an effort to change the subject.

'Naturally we have a carriage. Is there somewhere you wish to go?'

'To Briarwood Hall tomorrow afternoon. I have accepted an invitation to visit.'

'So Thomas Walford is showing an interest in you! I expect Marina will be displeased to learn that.'

'It has nothing to do with Thomas. What an odious mind you have! Amena wants to be friendly.'

Landers glared at her and then departed, and Victoria was in the act of going to her room when Elizabeth called to her. Ashley's wife came forward unsteadily, and Victoria caught the reek of whisky upon the older woman's breath.

'You and I ought to be friends, Victoria,' Elizabeth said.

'What makes you so certain of that?' Victoria spoke impatiently. 'You are married to Ashley and he hates the sight of me.'

'Married to Ashley! What a joke!' Elizabeth clutched at the heavy oaken rail along the edge of the gallery and Victoria reached out a supporting hand as she feared that the woman would pitch headlong over the top. 'Ashley is obsessed with inheriting from his father and wants to pass on the estate to his own son. The trouble is, he's married to me, and I cannot bear children.'

'Poor Elizabeth!' Victoria spoke involuntarily, realising a great deal from the poignant admission.

'Elizabeth!' Ashley appeared on the stairs, his harsh voice echoing in the vast, gloomy space of the hall. He came quickly to Victoria's side, thrusting her hand away from his wife's arm. 'How many times do I have to tell you to stop

drinking during the day? And stop raving like a lunatic or I'll have to teach you to keep your mouth shut.'

Victoria drew away in horror as Ashley thrust Elizabeth along the passage towards her room. She was tempted to go to Elizabeth's assistance, but realised that she could not interfere between a man and his wife. She turned to depart and was startled to find Landers almost behind her. He heard her involuntary gasp of shock and smiled.

'Not a pretty sight, is it?' he demanded bitterly. 'What a fool my eldest son is. Elizabeth will be a millstone around his neck for the rest of his life.'

The next afternoon when Victoria descended the steps to the waiting carriage she felt as if an intolerable burden had been lifted from her slender shoulders. The coachman held out his arm for her to grasp and she entered the dank vehicle, wrinkling her nose at the smell of the musty leather. When she looked back through the window as the carriage pulled away she fancied that she saw Landers watching her from a window, and she began to wish that she did not have to return.

But a sense of anticipation gripped her, and an unbidden picture of Thomas Walford came into her mind. Rain spattered against the carriage window, yet the countryside did not seem so alien and unfriendly now.

It was a six-mile drive to Briarwood Hall and the coach lurched along the muddy, rutted road. Victoria fought down a pang of impatience. She was aware that she needed friends badly. But could she tell the Walfords of the situation that existed at Seabrook?

Briarwood Hall was a large grey-stone house, square and solid, with creeper clinging to its walls. The coach slowed to enter the driveway, and Victoria felt a little knot of tension gather as they approached the Hall.

The front door was opened as the carriage halted at the foot of a flight of sandstone steps, and Thomas and Amena appeared in the doorway. The coachman helped Victoria to alight, and she was conscious only of pleasure at seeing Thomas again. Amena was smiling cheerfully, and Victoria was immediately impressed by the warm atmosphere of the Walford's home. When they entered the hall Amena adroitly took her leave and Victoria found herself the centre of Thomas's attention.

'How is your father?' she inquired, suddenly feeling diffident, aware that he was watching her with a gleam in his pale blue eyes.

'There's no change.' He was dressed in a dark suit and a white shirt with a high winged collar. 'And your grandfather?'

'Barely clinging to life. The doctor comes to see him every day but there is nothing he can do.'

'This feels like a happy house,' she commented.

'Let me show you over this place. I

am rightly proud of it.' He smiled as he met her gaze, and Victoria felt her pulses begin to race.

From the very first she and Thomas were comfortable with each other. They discovered that they liked the same kinds of furniture and decor, and there was no awkwardness between them. As Thomas showed her his domain a bond seemed to form between them and by the time they returned to the drawing room they were more like old friends than comparative strangers.

Amena was seated upon a couch before a blazing fire, reading. 'Hello,' she greeted, looking up and smiling. 'Finished the grand tour?'

'It's a beautiful house,' Victoria responded. 'I wish Seabrook was only half as bright.'

'It's not the house but the people in it,' Amena retorted, and Thomas smiled.

'May I ask what your plans are for Christmastide?' Amena asked as Victoria was preparing to leave later. 'You're surely not going to stay at Seabrook with the Radbournes.'

'I must admit the prospect is somewhat daunting, but I don't think I can make any plans at this time. I certainly don't want to spend the festive season with Landers and the others, but there is my grandfather to be considered.'

'Let's make tentative arrangements for you to come here,' Thomas suggested. 'There will be only Amena and I. We have no kinfolk apart from our father. I think you would enjoy our company.'

Victoria agreed, but there was a strange reluctance in the back of her mind as she took her leave shortly afterwards, and while she was being driven home she huddled under the rugs, thinking of Thomas and feeling excited because he had asked her to accompany him the next afternoon to Tregston to see the shops and stalls decorated for Christmas.

Seabrook was in darkness except for

a lantern over the front door when the coach churned to a halt in front of the steps. The door opened as she climbed the steps and Seldon appeared, correctly dressed and formal despite the lateness of the hour.

'I hope you've had an enjoyable time, Miss Victoria,' he said, taking her cloak and bonnet.

'Most enjoyable,' she responded. 'Thank you, Seldon. Is there any change in my grandfather's condition?'

'No, Miss.' Seldon excused himself and took her outer clothes into the cloakroom. Returning, he collected a lamp from the small table by the door. 'I'll light the way to your room before making a final check of the house, Miss. Would you like your maid?'

'No, thank you.' Victoria shook her head. 'I'm sorry if I've kept you from your bed, Seldon.'

'I'm happy that you have enjoyed yourself, Miss. I hope the Walfords will prove good and loyal friends.'

Victoria's last thought as she drifted into slumber was of the gentle expression on Thomas's face as he'd kissed her hand in farewell.

6

A terrible shriek that echoed through the night startled Victoria from her sleep and she sprang up in bed, staring around wildly as the echoes of the cry faded. Darkness surrounded her. The fire in the grate was dead. Silence closed in, and she could feel her heart thumping madly as she tried to guess what had happened. Hurriedly she lit the candle on her bedside table. Pulling on a dressing gown, she unlocked the door and, holding the candle high, peered fearfully along the corridor.

A sputtering candle threw uncertain light around the head of the stairs, and then Landers stepped into view. Victoria left her room and hurried towards him, moistening her lips as she drew within earshot.

'What was that cry?' she demanded, suddenly wondering if it had been intended to lure her out of the sanctuary of her room. More lights approached. Ashley was coming from his room, and Marina was a few yards behind him. Farther back along the corridor, Benjamin hovered in his doorway.

'Master Landers! You'd better come quickly,' Seldon called urgently from the hall.

Landers and Ashley hurried down the stairs into the dim stairwell. The dim yellow glow of Seldon's lamp revealed an inert figure stretched out in the hall, and Marina, coming silently to Victoria's side, uttered a gasp.

'That's Elizabeth! Was it her who cried out?' She did not wait for an answer but went hurrying down the stairs to her father and brother, who were now crouching beside Seldon. The butler was on his knees beside the crumpled figure.

'Is it Elizabeth?' Victoria asked as Marina came hurrying back up the stairs.

'It certainly is, and she's dead. Her neck is broken.' There was no emotion in Marina's harsh voice. 'I'm going back to bed. There's nothing anyone can do for her. My father says you'd better go back to bed also, and stay there until morning.'

Victoria shook her head as Marina departed, her gaze riveted upon the scene below. Ashley suddenly arose and crossed the hall to the library, carrying a lamp, and when he returned moments later he was holding a drink in one hand. He stood back, watching his father and Seldon bending over his dead wife, and drank repeatedly from the glass in his hand. Then he looked up and stared at Victoria, who shivered and turned away. She hurried to her room and slammed the door, bolted it securely and went back to bed.

But there was no more sleep for her! Horror filled her mind. Elizabeth was dead! The single thought pounded in her mind. Poor woman! No matter her failings, she had deserved better than

Ashley provided. She closed her eyes but sleep eluded her and although she drowsed from time to time she lay hollow-eyed until morning.

Daylight came slowly. Wind was howling dismally round the chimney-pots and rattling the windows when Daisy knocked at the door. Victoria admitted the girl. Daisy was crying, tears streaming down her face.

'Oh, Miss!' she gasped. 'Do you know what's happened? Miss Elizabeth is dead! She fell down the stairs in the night. Her neck was broken!'

Victoria could not rid her mind of the terrible shriek that had awakened her. She nodded silently as Daisy stared at her, and the maid broke into a spate of renewed sobbing.

'Oh, poor Mistress Elizabeth! She was a good woman when she first came here. It was Ashley drove her to this.'

'What do you mean?' Victoria demanded. 'What did Ashley do?'

'No-one would treat a dog the way he treated her,' Daisy cried. 'Mistress

Elizabeth didn't touch a drink when she first came here. Ashley drove her to it, and now she's dead. She must have thrown herself down the stairs to end her misery.'

'How can you say such a thing?' Victoria remonstrated. 'No matter what Ashley did, it was between the two of them. Elizabeth could have left if she were so unhappy.'

'No-one leaves the Radbournes, Miss, if they haven't a mind to let you go.' Daisy wrung her hands. 'It's a bad business, and there's worse to come, you mark my words.'

Victoria tried to get more from the distraught maid, but Daisy turned to the door.

'I'll get your hot water, Miss, and after this you'd better keep your door locked night and day.'

Victoria sat on the foot of her bed, thoughtful as she awaited Daisy's return, and then began to prepare to face the day, only half listening to the maid's doleful voice.

'I blame myself, Miss Victoria,' Daisy said tearfully. 'Who would have thought this could happen? I put her to bed last night. I did that most nights because she wasn't able to look after herself by that time of the day. I'm sure Master Landers blames me for what happened.'

'Why should he?' Victoria demanded. 'You did settle her down for the night, didn't you?'

'Yes, Miss, and tucked her in so she couldn't fall out. It wouldn't be the first time Mistress Elizabeth fell out of bed, I can tell you.'

'Did she ever get out of bed after being tucked in?' Victoria frowned as she asked the question.

'There was no telling what she might do when the drink was in her. I've found her wandering around the house in complete darkness. Gave me a bad scare more than once, Miss.'

'You have nothing to reproach yourself for,' Victoria consoled. 'Did they send for the doctor last night?'

'Yes, Miss, and he said there would have to be an inquiry. He told Master Landers not to worry for he would give evidence. It's a clear case of accidental death.'

Victoria was filled with speculation as she finished her toilette. There were niggling doubts in the back of her mind, and when she went down to breakfast she paused on the bottom stair and gazed at the spot where Elizabeth had lain. The woman's trailing shriek of horror resounded in her mind until she felt like screaming in protest at the doubts assailing her. But she controlled herself and went to the kitchen, passing into the scullery where the boot-boy was already at work in his small cupboard of a room.

'Your shoes aren't cleaned yet, Miss,' he said, looking up and pulling his forelock when he saw Victoria.

'I'm in no hurry,' she replied, speaking gently, for he seemed in awe of her. 'My riding boots have a brown stain on them that I somehow picked up last week. I didn't leave them out for cleaning, so perhaps you could fetch them from my room and try to clean them. That stain looks like brown paint.'

'Then you've been round the old mansion, Miss.' The boy grinned. 'Master Ashley got some on his boots, too.'

'Did he?' Victoria narrowed her eyes as she considered that snippet of information. She was still of the opinion that someone had been in the old mansion when she and Benjamin sheltered in it from the rain. Could it have been Ashley? That beam had not fallen accidentally. Of that she was certain.

'I'm not allowed in the bedrooms, Miss,' the boy said, interrupting her thoughts. 'If you'll give your boots to Daisy she'll hand them to me.'

Victoria thanked him and departed, entering the breakfast room to find Landers there, looking worried. His face was taut with a sharp expression, and his dark eyes gleamed with an inner passion. He was evidently under a great strain.

'There will be a policeman here this morning,' he announced. 'Just a routine inquiry. I'm trying to keep you out of it. You were not involved. Daisy was the last one to see Elizabeth alive. It's a clear case of death by misadventure.'

'How is Grandfather this morning?' Victoria asked, changing the subject.

'No change! But you are to stay away from him.' Landers turned and departed abruptly, closing the door with a bang.

Victoria merely picked at her breakfast, and afterwards entered the library. She selected a book and tried to settle to read. As time passed, she felt, irrationally, that she was being watched, and glanced around, half expecting to find that someone had entered the room unnoticed. But, of course, she was alone. The feeling persisted and she became restless. Getting to her feet, she paced to and fro for a few moments. At the far end of the room she turned toward the big window, and noticed a small shower of dust particles floating down from the ornate ceiling. Frowning, she traced the shower to its source. It seemed to be coming from the intricate mouldings around the chandelier. Then she heard a dull thud from the room overhead.

Hurrying into the hall, she saw the door of Landers' bedroom opening on the gallery, directly above the library. They passed on the stairs. Victoria went to the gallery and turned to see Landers talking to Seldon, who was opening the front door. Landers went into the library and Seldon ushered in a tall, thin man who was dressed in a dark suit and stiff white collar.

Glancing around to ensure that she was not being observed, Victoria then slipped into Landers' room and closed the door. She imagined that the chandelier in the library was almost directly beneath the open fireplace and crossed to the stone surround, peering intently at the floorboards adjoining it.

One of them seemed loose, and when she tugged at it she was surprised to find that it lifted quite easily.

Horror filled her when she looked down and discovered that a small peep-hole gave her a narrow but perfect view of the library beneath. By moving her head she could see the stranger in front of the fire and Landers seated in the chair which she had recently vacated. She could hear their voices quite clearly. Landers was describing how Elizabeth had been most troublesome with her drinking habits, reporting that Ashley had, on several occasions, prevented her from injuring herself while under the influence of liquor. She heard him address the newcomer as Inspector!

Victoria replaced the board carefully and went to the door, opening it a fraction to check the passage, and when she saw that it was deserted she departed hurriedly, closing the door softly and walking quickly to her own room.

Once in her sanctuary she leaned

against the door and looked around carefully. Since her arrival she had, on several occasions, sensed that she was being watched secretly. She began a meticulous search of the walls. When she found a cunningly concealed peep-hole in the picture frame she was aghast. Applying an eye to the hole she discovered that she could not see into the next room, but imagined that the other end of the peep-hole was covered.

Was there no limit to Landers' deviousness? But more than that, what had really happened to Elizabeth? Had she simply fallen down the stairs? Or had she jumped or been pushed?

A strange hush seemed to envelop the house. The inspector departed without asking to see her, and it was after lunch when Victoria heard the grating of wheels outside and recalled that Thomas had arranged to collect and take her into Tregston to see the sights. She hurried down the staircase as he was being admitted by Seldon.

The butler was telling Thomas about

Elizabeth when Victoria joined them, and she saw his features pale at the grim news. But at that moment Ashley emerged from the library and gazed at Thomas with undisguised hatred. Coming forward to confront them, he thrust out his jaw as he stared hard at Victoria.

'Have you no respect for the dead?' he demanded. 'My wife is not dead twenty-four hours and you're going out socialising with a neighbour.'

Victoria caught her breath, shocked by his outburst. 'You think I have no respect for the dead?' she demanded. 'Why, you had no respect for your wife when she was alive.'

Ashley came forward a pace, lifting a hand as if to strike Victoria, but Thomas stepped forward, thrusting his tall, powerful figure between them.

'That will be quite enough, Ashley,' he snapped. 'I will accept that you are labouring under a great strain, but don't ever speak to Victoria like that again.'

It was fortunate that Landers appeared from the drawing room, attracted by Ashley's loud voice, and he came immediately to his son's side.

'Go to your room, Ashley,' he commanded harshly, but his gaze was upon Victoria's flushed face as he spoke. He waited for his son to turn away before continuing. 'I would go out this afternoon if I were you,' he said. 'Elizabeth's death has been a shock for you also, and an outing will do you good.'

Victoria suppressed a sigh and turned to Thomas. 'Shall we go?' she asked.

'With pleasure,' he retorted, and Seldon hurried to fetch her cloak and bonnet.

Victoria sighed with relief as they stepped outside into the dry, cold afternoon, but as they descended the steps to the waiting carriage a clattering of hooves sounded upon the gravel and she glanced to the right to see Marina riding into view around the house from the stables. The quick expression of hatred and jealousy which came to Marina's face when she spotted them was a mute warning of total enmity, and Victoria entered the carriage with a feeling of impending doom enveloping her.

7

They drove to Tregston, a small market town, and, as it was December, Christmas trade was beginning to pick up and there were signs that the festive season was approaching. When they left the carriage to walk through the town, Victoria pressed close to Thomas, who took hold of her arm, and they joined the thronging people around the stalls in the market.

Dusk set in early and the market was illuminated by the glare of naphtha lamps. The whole scene was one of make-believe for Victoria, and her face was flushed, eyes gleaming with pleasure as they enjoyed the hurly-burly and cheerfulness of the people. It surprised her, too, when so many people spoke to her, clearly aware of her identity and why she was in the locality.

But finally it was time to return to the coach, and they left behind the bright lights to jolt along the bad road in their musty carriage. They were in near darkness, with just a slight reflection entering from the guttering lamps fixed to the sides of the vehicle. Victoria experienced a mood of wistfulness and sighed.

'Are you unhappy, Victoria?' Thomas asked, merely a dark shadow at her side.

'Unhappy?' she echoed. 'No. In fact, I don't think I have ever enjoyed myself more.' She paused and compressed her lips. 'If only poor Elizabeth hadn't fallen! It's a shocking business.'

'Yes.' He nodded. 'The situation for you at the moment is quite unsettling, and apart from the miserable reception you've received at Seabrook, there is the matter of your inheritance. I am concerned for you, Victoria. I have heard the rumours of what Landers did to your father many years ago, and if there is any truth in that then you could be in some considerable danger.'

'Thank you for your concern,' she replied, suppressing a sigh. 'Elizabeth was trying to tell me something yesterday, but because she was in her usual state of inebriation I didn't pay much heed. Now she is dead! I can't help wondering if what happened to her was not an accident.'

'I must confess that the same kind of thoughts have been passing through the back of my mind,' Thomas said. 'And if that is the case then you ought not stay another night alone in Seabrook.'

'I don't think I would be in any real danger until after Landers became certain that he will not inherit. He would not risk his life putting me out of the way if the estate went to him later. Being the schemer that he is, surely he would wait and get his facts right before acting!'

'I am counting on that premise being correct,' Thomas said gravely. 'But I am very much concerned by all this, I can tell you. I wish I knew how to advise you for the best.'

She was sorry when they finally reached Seabrook, and before Thomas opened the door of the carriage he clasped her hands and squeezed them gently.

'Try not to worry too much,' he advised softly. 'With your permission I shall call on you frequently in future. Someone has got to watch out for your interests, and Amena is quite concerned about you.' He paused. 'So am I, of course!'

'That's very kind of you.' She smiled. 'Knowing that you and Amena are in the background relieves my fears a great deal. Thank you, Thomas.'

'It is my pleasure,' he retorted.

The coachman opened the door of the carriage and Thomas alighted, holding out an arm to her. She stepped to the ground, and would have been happier if the afternoon had just begun. The door of the house was opened as they ascended the steps, and Seldon appeared in the doorway.

'Won't you come in for a moment?' Victoria invited.

'I would like nothing better.' He smiled regretfully. 'But now I have to attend to certain other matters. However, I'll call upon you tomorrow, if I may.'

'Please do. I shall be very happy to see you.'

Seldon smiled as he took her cloak and bonnet. 'It does seem as if Cornwall agrees with you, Miss,' he observed, noting her glistening eyes and eager expression. 'I am relieved that you are now making friends.'

'Then you are a fool, Seldon,' Marina spoke harshly from the doorway of the drawing room, a riding crop in her hand which she banged impatiently against her leather riding boot. 'It's quite easy to see where your sympathies lie, and obviously loyalty is not one of your virtues.' She came forward a few steps. 'You are no doubt aware that my father and the rest of us will be tossed out of here the moment my grandfather dies. Is that why you are playing up to this newcomer? You are ingratiating yourself in order to make your position secure. Well, Grandfather is still alive, and I'm tempted to have my father dismiss you before he loses his authority.'

'Don't be so obnoxious, Marina!' Victoria cut in. 'Why pick on someone who cannot defend himself? Seldon is merely being polite to me. In fact I have never met a more competent servant. But you are not so concerned with Seldon as with my activities. So don't victimise him because you cannot take me to task.'

'You!' Marina sneered. 'What do I care about you?'

'That's just the point.' Victoria paused while Seldon withdrew. Then she faced up to her cousin, who paused in the centre of the hall, still swishing her riding crop. 'It's Thomas you're upset about, isn't it? I can see your jealousy.'

'You've come here for the estate.'

Marina's eyes glittered. 'But you won't get it.' She came forward a step, her mouth twisted with emotion, swinging the riding crop as if she would like to whip Victoria.

'There's no need for raised voices,' Landers called sharply, and Victoria saw him descending the stairs. He always seemed to be around when one of his family was getting argumentative, Victoria thought. 'Go into the library, Marina,' he rapped. 'I want to talk to you.'

'I'll stay here and have my say,' the girl retorted.

'You'll do as I say or I'll take that crop to you.' Landers came off the bottom step and grabbed his daughter's arm, but his gaze was on Victoria, and she fearlessly met his eyes. His expression hardened as he turned away, forcibly escorting the fuming Marina into the library. Then Ashley and Benjamin appeared on the stairs. They passed Victoria silently and also entered the library, closing the door with a thud. Victoria wondered what they were going to discuss, and shook her head slowly as she went up to her room.

Dinner that evening threatened to be an ordeal, but passed quite uneventfully, Victoria found, although Marina could not control her feelings. It was obvious that Landers had spoken strongly to his family, and each of them although not trying to be civil was not openingly insulting. That night Victoria slept easily for the first time at Seabrook, and during the days that followed there seemed a general lessening of the tension that had abounded earlier.

Elizabeth was buried, and Victoria was not invited to the funeral. She stood at a window and watched the cortege depart for the little church, and was saddened because she had been unable to make friends with the woman. But she had her own life to worry about, and, when Thomas arrived later, she revelled in his company. They sat in the drawing room, and there seemed to be a quite different atmosphere in the house because Landers and his family were absent. She realised that she was being drawn towards Thomas, liking his quiet, gentlemanly manner and genteel attitude. They became quite friendly and laughed together a great deal.

Ashley never attempted to molest her now, and whenever he passed her around the house she could only wonder what was in his mind. But she was not deceived by his air of apparent unconcern. She was alert every minute she spent in the house.

Her grandfather's condition remained unchanged, according to the reports she received from Landers, who would not permit her to see the old man. A nurse was brought in to care for him, but she refused to talk to Victoria at all about the patient's condition, referring her to Landers when she did inquire.

'Are you making any plans for Christmas, Landers?' Victoria asked when she saw him in the hall. She was awaiting the arrival of the Walford carriage to convey her to Briarwood.

'Christmas?' He seemed startled by the question, and frowned.

'It's Christmas next week.' she prompted, wondering if, even at this late hour, he might relent and become friendly.

'There'll be no festivities in this house,' he said sharply. 'My father is lying next to death's door. One day is the same as another to me.' He paused, aware by her changing expression that he had hurt her. 'You keep Christmas any way you want, and leave me to do the same.'

'I'm aware that Grandfather is seriously ill,' she said, 'but there is nothing I can do about it. You are not exactly grief-stricken yourself! So I do not feel guilt, and I expect to be at Briarwood for the twelve days of Christmas.'

'That is good news.' Landers smiled thinly. 'At least we shall be able to look upon Seabrook as ours for one more year's end.'

The sound of a carriage approaching

alerted Victoria, and she sighed with relief, for it heralded Thomas's arrival, and Landers smiled cynically as she turned towards the door when Seldon appeared.

She left the mansion feeling depressed. But upon entering the coach with Thomas her spirits began to rise.

'I wish I didn't have to come back here while Landers and his family are still here,' she said as Thomas called out to the coachman to drive on.

'At least you can leave it for the twelve days of Christmas,' he responded.

'Yes.' She nodded. 'In view of the situation I'll gladly spend the Yuletide season at Briarwood.'

'Good.' Thomas leaned forward and took her hand. 'I understand how you feel, Victoria, and I wish I could do something constructive to help.'

Victoria suppressed a sigh as she gazed from the carriage window. The first snow of winter was falling, and strands of fog were clinging to the trees. The hooves of the horses were strangely muted and the grating wheels swished through the slush that abounded.

'I do hope this situation will clear itself up very soon,' Thomas said quietly as they entered Briarwood. 'I can see that you are troubled and it pains me to know there is little I can do to help.'

'You are doing more than anyone could expect,' she responded. 'I just hope that I won't have a dampening effect upon your household during Christmas.' She could not help wondering exactly what was in his mind concerning her. She sensed that he liked her, but he never spoke of his personal feelings, and never seemed to have any association with other women — not even Marina. Her heart ached as she longed to get to know him better.

'Come and help us put up the holly and the ivy around the hall,' he said. 'Amena has been impatiently awaiting your arrival.'

She smiled and nodded and they entered the house, laughing together. As usual, the moment she crossed the threshold all her cares seemed to drop away. But this time the influence of Seabrook seemed to cling to her mind, malignant, brooding and dull, and she could not settle happily to anything. When she was on her way back to Seabrook later her fears returned even more strongly, and her heart seemed to quail when the carriage halted in front of the forbidding building.

Entering the house, she paused in the hall for Seldon to take her outer clothes, and then began to make her way up to her room. But Marina was waiting in the shadowy gallery, and startled Victoria by emerging unexpectedly from a nook and laying a hand upon her arm.

'Shhh!' Marina pressed a warning finger to her lips. 'As much as I hate you for playing up to Thomas, I can't let them do what they have in mind. Listen to me and don't interrupt. I have to get back to my room without being seen. Get out of the house now. They are planning to do you a mischief. I heard my father and Ashley talking. Fenton will be dead soon and they must prevent you from inheriting.'

'What?' Victoria clutched at Marina's arm, but the woman jerked away and flitted along the gallery like a wraith.

Fear filled Victoria's breast as she peered around, feeling the hostility of the cold surroundings filtering into her trembling body. Marina disappeared, and Victoria was alone with merely a guttering candle on a side table giving off a very dim light. Silence closed in about her and her skin prickled.

Were they really going to try and get rid of her? She thought of Thomas in his carriage, only a few minutes back along the road to Briarwood, and wished that she had accepted his offer to stay at his home until the situation here had clarified itself. She turned silently with the intention of going down to the hall, but before she reached the staircase a door slammed somewhere at her back, and she hurried into cover behind the curtains at one of the windows.

The next instant footsteps went hurrying by, and she peered out fearfully to see Benjamin descending the stairs. Shivers darted along her spine. She had to make an effort to leave the cover of the curtains, and her first instinct was to go to the cloakroom for her outdoor clothes and then make her way to Briarwood Hall and Thomas. But commonsense prevailed, for she was keenly aware that she would probably lose her way in the deep snowdrifts and freeze to death long before morning.

She went to her room and locked herself in. For a long time she could do nothing but sit by the fire and listen fearfully for any unnatural sound. But tiredness assailed her and she got under the covers on the bed with her clothes on. The candle guttered at times, but Victoria could not fight off her tiredness, and slowly sank back and lost her senses. When she awoke with a start it was to hear the maid at the door, and relief filled her when she realised that morning had come.

As she changed and attended to her toilette, Victoria pondered Marina's warning. But in the cold light of the morning she could not believe that Landers would go so far to gain control of the estate, and by the time she was ready to go down to breakfast she had decided that she had nothing to fear until she actually inherited the estate. Surely Landers would wait until then!

But she checked the lock on her door, and then went to the windows to look over their catches. Her breath caught in her throat when she discovered that the metal catch on the big window was loose, and there were some marks on the surrounding woodwork which indicated that a sharp-pointed tool had been used to weaken the catch. She found Seldon in the hall and explained the situation.

'I'll look into it, Miss Victoria, and have the footman effect some repair work,' he promised.

'Thank you,' she replied, and realised that she could not afford to relax her vigilance, but she was determined not to be frightened out of the house.

Miss Maitland approached Victoria in the hall. The housekeeper was holding a book which she handed to Victoria, who frowned, and the older woman smiled.

'I was up in the attic earlier, Miss Victoria, and came across this book. It belonged to your father when he was a boy. There are many interesting things up there, relics of the past. The attic was your father's favourite playground. There are drawings that he did on some of the walls.'

'Really?' Victoria was immediately interested. 'Then I must go and look. I remember Father telling me about the attic, but since my arrival I haven't been able to think about it.'

Miss Maitland handed her a key. 'I keep the attic locked these days. Too many valuables stored up there have either been broken or have gone missing. Please return the key when you've finished with it.'

'I will, and thank you.' Victoria ascended the stairs, but paused outside the door of her Grandfather's room. She deliberated for a moment, then gently opened the door and peered in. Her grandfather lay inert in bed, eyes closed, asleep or still in the coma. She saw the nurse in a corner of the room and eased back and closed the door silently. Her thoughts were harsh as she considered the past and her dead father. Landers had a lot to answer for!

Ashley appeared in the corridor and Victoria, not wanting him to know where she was going, went on to her own room. He passed her, a surly expression on his face, and it was not until she was safely behind her own door that she realised the attic key was clasped in her hand where he could easily have seen it. She waited five minutes, then went back to the stairs and ascended to the top floor. The silence which filled the narrow stairway was heavy and seemed not to have been disturbed for many years.

The key grated in the lock and the door swung open. Victoria peered inside, and experienced an uncanny sensation of excitement and nervousness. There was a big square skylight overhead, but the sky above was grey and ominous with clouds. She looked around curiously, not knowing what to expect. There was a great stack of boxes against the far wall, looking as if they had become fixtures. A wardrobe with its doors agape contained dresses and gowns that must have been the very height of fashion at least 50 years before.

Victoria entered, leaving the door open. The skylight rattled under the force of the wind, and an eerie moaning sound played havoc with her nerves. She saw some indistinct drawings on the wall beside the window, and crossed the room for a closer look. Her father had loved horses, and had possessed artistic ability. When she saw that the drawings consisted of horses a pang touched her breast for she knew intuitively that her father had drawn them. She began to browse through the attic, her thoughts occupied with the past.

A terrific crash made her jump. She was startled and clasped her hands to her breast. The door had slammed! She stared at it, listening to the diminishing echoes while her pulses raced and her breath stuck in her constricted throat. Shadows seemed to have crawled into the corners of the large room, and she narrowed her eyes. Then she recovered her composure and hurried to the door, grasping its handle and throwing her weight against it.

The door would not budge! She paused, trying to fight down the fear that tried insidiously to panic her. She tried the handle again, exerting considerable strength, believing that the wind had somehow caused a draught which had slammed the door. But it did not yield an inch. She tried to force the handle but it remained obdurate, and then she froze, for from the other side of the door a hoarse chuckling sounded. It was harsh and animal-like, and scared her. She shrank back, hands clenched, breath caught in her throat. Blood pounded at her temples and there was a stabbing pang in her breast.

'Who's there?' she called tremulously, and almost sank to her knees in fright when the door shook under a ferocious battering. There was a bolt on the inside and she reached forward instinctively and slid it home. The next instant the handle was turned on the outside and the door creaked and shivered as great pressure was exerted against it.

Victoria pressed a hand to her mouth, frightened, bemused. She leaned against the door, hoping that her slender weight would keep it closed. Who could be outside? Landers? Ashley? Benjamin? Had they been watching her, looking for just such an opportunity as this?

Silence came suddenly, and it seemed more frightening than the noise. She strained her ears for unnatural sounds as strands of fear crept into her mind. Rapid footsteps suddenly began to pound away down the stairs. Then the silence was resumed, heavier, more overpowering.

Victoria sagged against the door, her nerve almost shattered. She gasped for breath, dizzy from the emotional shock she had received. Her heart was pounding erratically, and for several awful moments she feared that she might lose her senses, for the big room seemed to tilt and whirl. But by degrees she regained her equilibrium and the world returned to normal.

She drew a deep breath. Her hands were shaking uncontrollably. She clasped them and tried to steady herself, then began to upbraid herself for foolishly arriving at such a disadvantage. She had presented her enemies, whoever they might be, with a perfect opportunity to get at her!

The silence dragged at her nerves. She checked that the bolt was secure. She could not get out but they could not get in at her and she was bound to be missed before very long. Miss Maitland knew she had come here. She frowned. A disconcerting thought struck her. Miss Maitland had given her the attic key and put into her head the thought of coming here to the top of the house. Had Landers compelled that frail, old lady to fall in with his wishes?

She pressed an ear against the door but heard nothing for long minutes. Her imagination was running riot, thrusting up fears that made her weak at the knees. Then she heard footsteps ascending, and Daisy's voice calling, strangely muffled by the thick door.

'Miss Victoria, are you here? Miss Maitland sent me to attend you.'

Victoria withdrew the bolt, and to her surprise the door opened immediately. She peered out, not knowing what to expect, and came face to face with the maid.

'Miss Victoria!' the girl cried. 'It's naughty of you to come up here alone. I wouldn't even if I was ordered! There are parts of this house that give me the creeps! Aren't you afraid?'

It took all of Victoria's willpower to present a casual manner. She forced a smile although her pulses were still racing. 'Why should I be afraid?' she demanded. 'This was my father's home, the place where he was born. No, I'm not afraid, and no-one is going to scare me off!'

She emerged from the attic and locked the door, then handed the key to Daisy with instructions for it to be returned to the housekeeper. As she descended the stairs to the hall she vowed that never again would she be so careless, and she would say nothing of the incident to anyone, not even Thomas. It had taught her a timely lesson, and for that at least she could be thankful . . .

On Christmas Eve she wrapped the presents she had bought for Thomas and Amena and packed the clothes she would need at Briarwood. After lunch she waited rather impatiently in the library for the Walford coach to collect her, and when it arrived she departed with relief filling her. Tench, the coachman, helped her into the vehicle, and as it drew away she looked out at the mansion, half-wishing that she did not have to return. Seabrook was practically in darkness, cold and cheer-less. A shiver tremored through her and she frowned and averted her face quickly from the bleak scene, not wanting to think of the grim past and all the hopelessness that had evolved from the Radbourne family. Despon-dence filled her as she was conveyed to Briarwood Hall.

8

When Victoria arrived at Briarwood she found light blazing from most of the windows and the front door standing wide open. There was the sound of many voices in the hall, she half-paused in some confusion, feeling that she could not face company in her present mood. Then Thomas appeared, outlined in the doorway, and she drew a deep breath, tried to overpower the struggling emotions in her breast, and forced a smile. Thomas came forward to take her hands, and she laughed, driving from her mind all thoughts of Seabrook.

'Victoria!' There was no mistaking the pleasure in Thomas's soft voice. 'At last! I've been on tenterhooks, afraid that you would cry off at the last moment. But now you're here nothing can make me let you go again until

Twelfth Night, and even then I shall protest if you want to leave, I promise you. Come in! Amena is busy with our guests. There are many people I want you to meet and who are all eager to meet you. This will indeed be a Christmas to remember.'

As he spoke, Thomas drew her across the threshold. A maid came forward to take her bonnet and fur-trimmed cloak. Victoria was reminded of Seldon. Thomas brushed a flake of snow from her cheek, and Victoria felt a warm glow suffuse her. Thoughts of Seabrook faded from her mind and animation began to flow through her. The hall was crowded with young people, and their voices were raised in an excited hubbub of noise. Thomas began to introduce her to his friends, and Victoria seemed to climb upon a carousel of unreality. She could not afterwards remember any of the names that were mentioned, and faces came and went in an unceasing parade. But afterwards she had time to rethink her first impressions. Later she was confronted by Amena.

'I'm so glad you're here,' the girl confided. 'All these people are our very good friends, but you have become something special in the few short weeks we've known you.'

Victoria smiled, feeling happy for the first time. Thomas had the duties of host to perform in his father's absence, and she sat to one side on a window seat, watching the late-comers arriving. She was mentally composed now, and Seabrook was like a bad dream in the back of her mind — something which could be temporarily forgotten.

Thomas kept coming back to her, and brought a succession of eager young people to keep her company while he attended to his duties. She forced herself to enter into the spirit of Christmas, which pervaded the house, and presently she was led by Thomas through the dining room to the punch room, where servants brought wine in beautiful Venetian glasses, and in no time at all Victoria was the centre of attention, answering countless questions about her life in America.

Time seemed to lose its significance and events developed in quick succession. They were called into the dining room for supper, and Victoria counted 32 guests around the long oak table that was tastefully laid with beautiful cut glass and gleaming silver dishes. Thomas sat at the head of the table with Victoria at his right.

The food was excellently served; beef and lamb, suckling pig, a boar's head and enormous pies, all washed down with plentiful wine and spiced ale, and the conversation continued unabated. Afterwards Amena led the ladies to the drawing room, where the huge tree that Victoria had so painstakingly helped to decorate dominated the far corner, aglow with small candles and glistening with tinsel.

Later they rejoined the gentlemen and sang carols. But Victoria was especially pleased when they entered the ballroom at the rear end of the hall and five musicians began to play. There was some dancing, and Thomas ensured he had the opportunity of taking her into his arms. He whirled her around under the glittering chandeliers to the strains of a waltz, and she felt her senses spin as she glimpsed so many strange faces. The gallery which surrounded the ballroom was alive with non-dancers, and the clink of glasses sounded sharp in the background, mingling with the never-ceasing voices.

'You look flushed but extremely happy,' Thomas remarked as the waltz came to an end. 'For the first time since I've known you I believe you are really carefree, except for that afternoon when I took you into Tregston.'

'That is a memory I shall always treasure,' she assured him with a smile. 'I am happy, Thomas, and most grateful that you have opened your house to me.'

'I have opened more than my house to you,' he answered.

Victoria caught her breath, and, as

her brown eyes widened, her expression of surprise was so evident that Thomas chuckled. She felt as if she were living in a dream: the guests, the music, the brilliance of her surroundings and the fact that Christmas was upon them.

When the clock struck 11 the revelling ended and the guests departed. Carriages lined the driveway and Thomas and Amena stood at the door, shaking hands with each of their friends, wishing them all a merry Christmas. When the door was closed there was just Thomas, Amena and Victoria in the hall, and the silence that closed in upon them seemed intolerable after all the merry-making.

'Well,' Thomas commented, sighing heavily. 'We have passed the Eve of Christmas in our usual fashion and this has been the most enjoyable I can ever recall. But now starts the twelve days of Christmas, and they will be very hectic.' He glanced at Victoria, a smile on his lips. 'Do you think you'll be able to stand the pace?'

She nodded eagerly, smiling. If this was a foretaste of what life would be like in England then she wanted Christmas to last for ever.

But time can never stand still even if events were the most perfect in the world, Victoria discovered. Christmas morning dawned crisp and cold, with snow flurrying across the countryside. When Victoria awakened to the tapping that came at the door she immediately imagined that she was back at Seabrook and Daisy was outside with the morning tea. But the door was opened and Amena appeared, wearing a scarlet dressing gown secured around her waist with a silken cord.

'A Merry Christmas, Vicky,' she cried excitedly, hurrying across the room to sit upon the bed and hug Victoria, who quickly sat up.

'Merry Christmas, Amena,' Victoria responded, recollecting herself. She smiled ruefully. 'For a moment I feared I was back at Seabrook.'

'Is it really as bad as all that?' Amena

stared into Victoria's face, her blue eyes filled with calculation. 'We really must do something about this situation, you know. We mention it, make a few observations, and then forget about it again. But you're caught up in the middle of all this, and if Thomas and I don't put ourselves out to change things then no-one else will. You don't know another soul in this country, do you?'

Victoria sighed. 'No-one,' she said. 'If I disappeared today, no-one here would ever give a second thought to me.'

'Thomas and I would,' Amena said emphatically. 'We will get something done. Now come and get up. There are gifts under the tree.'

Victoria slipped out of bed and quickly donned a dressing gown, then pushed her feet into fur-trimmed slippers. They descended to the drawing room, where Thomas was waiting in front of the Christmas tree, fully dressed. He was still lighting the candles on the tinselled branches, but he turned expectantly as the door was burst open by an exuberant Amena.

'Merry Christmas,' he greeted, coming forward to meet Victoria.

'Merry Christmas!' The phrase echoed round the room, and for an awful moment Victoria had a vision of what Seabrook Mansion must be like at this precise moment. But she fought off the nightmare and concentrated upon these very good friends.

'Now, we mustn't open all the gifts immediately,' Amena said excitedly as she hurried to the tree and began to search through the carefully wrapped packages lying beneath its spreading branches. 'Just the ones we've bought one another.' She selected one and held it out to Victoria. 'To Victoria, with great fondness, from Thomas,' she announced.

Victoria smiled as she accepted the gift, and her dark gaze went to Thomas's intent face. He was smiling, his blue eyes filled with pleasure.

'Open it,' he suggested. 'I heard you

remark last week that you liked what is in there.'

Victoria gazed at the small package with curiosity, and Thomas chuckled. But Amena had found Victoria's present to Thomas, and handed it over. When they each had a gift to unwrap there was the rustling of paper, and Victoria felt her pleasure growing. She glanced at Thomas's lean face and saw his eyes shine when he opened the small box which contained a jewelled pin for his cravat. She opened her gift to discover that he had bought her the earrings she pointed out to him during their trip to Tregston. A gasp escaped her as she gazed at them.

'Isn't this the perfect Christmas?' Amena demanded. 'It has always been so quiet other years. But now we have our own special friend.'

Victoria smiled, thinking of all the friends who had been present the night before. But none of them had stayed overnight. She looked into Thomas's face and saw a promise for the future in his eyes. Her heartbeat quickened as he took her hands in his and smiled down at her.

'I hope this will be the first of many happy times we shall spend together,' he said softly.

'This is the one I shall always remember,' she replied.

'We have to go to church this morning,' Thomas said, 'and then make a round of the village. My father is Lord of the Manor, but as he is ill I have to deputise for him.'

They were too excited to eat breakfast, and afterwards the carriage was summoned and they set out for the church. Snow had fallen during the night to a depth of several inches, and when they reached the church they found the villagers out in force, scraping snow away from the front of their homes. Boys were fighting with snowballs and a line of toboggans was swishing down the hill beyond the village.

After church they took the carriage

back to Briarwood, and Victoria's cheeks were rosy as they alighted in front of the house. They went into the drawing room to await dinner. Thomas poured wine for them and they toasted the day and each other.

Victoria had fallen under the spell of the festive season and her proximity to Thomas filled her with happiness. She discovered that no matter where she looked, her gaze repeatedly wandered back to his face, and she realised that her emotions were undergoing a tremendous upheaval. She had fancied, the previous evening, that she was falling in love with Thomas, and this day of days seemed to corroborate that suspicion.

Dinner was a regal affair, with turkey, beautifully carved, and all the trimmings. After the meal they retired to the drawing room, where bowls of nuts and fruit were placed on a small side table. Victoria sank into a deep armchair as Amena put a shovelful of chestnuts on the log fire. Thomas poured more wine.

Holding up his glass he proposed:

'A Merry Christmas, and may God bless all those in need.'

It was a perfect day for Victoria, sitting in Thomas's company completely relaxed and at ease. Now she had not a care in the world and did not even think of Seabrook. When darkness fell there was just the leaping flames of the big log fire, made of oak and elm and sweet-smelling bog turf, and the tiny candles on the Christmas tree, to give low illumination to the large drawing room. A sense of peacefulness and goodwill prevailed, and Victoria's heart was soothed with pleasure.

By midnight they were wearied and reluctantly ended the festivities. Victoria retired with an easy mind, thankful that she did not have to bolt her door, but lay awake for a long time in the darkness, thinking over the long day and recalling everything of significance that had been said. She was certain that Thomas was attracted to her! She had never felt so happy.

Boxing Day proved to be a contrast in every way. The morning started quietly and they sat and chatted until lunch. But during the afternoon the carriage was summoned and they set out to visit the home of one of Thomas's friends. The serenity and intimacy of Christmas Day were gone. Now was the time for parties, and Victoria found herself caught up in a whirl of gaiety that made her breathless. Boxing Day passed, and they did not return to Briarwood until the small hours, the horses having to struggle through deep snowdrifts. Victoria fell exhausted into her bed and lay dreamless until Milly called her later in the morning.

But there was no respite. Day after day the carriage was summoned during the afternoon and they were whisked off to one or another large house that was ablaze with light and colour and throbbing with music. When Victoria finally protested at the fast pace, Amena laughed merrily.

'We wait all year for this,' she said gaily. 'Make the most of it, Vicky. Gather ye rosebuds while ye may.'

'We'll be holding the very last party of the season here on Twelfth Night,' Thomas said. 'And if we don't slow down a bit then we'll not be on our feet when we have to act as the hosts.'

Victoria mentally agreed, and found herself alone with Thomas at Briarwood the next evening while Amena went alone to the home of one of their friends. They sat in the drawing room after tea, the curtains drawn against the chill night, the log fire blazing and only the tree lights on. Victoria sighed heavily as she relaxed, and Thomas, beside her on the couch, glanced intently at her.

'Weary of all the revelling, Vicky?' he asked softly.

'One can get too much of a good thing,' she replied.

'I agree, and, for my part, I'd rather be here alone with you tonight than at the Dersingham party. Do you realise that we have known each other almost two months?'

'Time doesn't seem to have any meaning these days, but I'll never forget our first meeting.'

'Nor I.' He shook his head, eyes suddenly narrowed. 'Apart from the coachman who was killed, I'm haunted by the sight of your face as I helped you out of the coach.'

'But it was very dark then,' she protested.

'I could see well enough that you were the girl I had been waiting for.' He leaned towards her and gazed into her eyes. 'We were thrown together, Vicky, and I believe it is what Fate intended. I have never met another girl who even remotely compares with you, and I'm not talking merely of beauty. Your character, your manner, everything about you is just perfect. Although I am bound by my father's wishes to marry another, I must confess that I am in love with you, and have been from the very first moment.'

Victoria caught her breath, startled

by his words, confused by his declaration of love and the admission that he was bound to marry someone else. 'I don't understand,' she faltered.

'I'm sorry. I ought to have told you about it some other way. But there isn't another way. I can tell that you care about me, and I want to let myself go as Nature intends lovers to do. But it has long been the desire of my father that I should wed whoever is suitable from Seabrook in order to bring the two estates together. That's why I've been pestered by Marina, although it is the thought of being the mistress of Briarwood that intrigues her, I'm certain, and not myself.'

'Oh!' Victoria clenched her hands. 'That's why Marina has been so certain that she would have you. But you must be aware that I am here in England at my grandfather's request so that I can inherit Seabrook.'

'I've heard rumours.' He shrugged. 'But there have always been rumours about Seabrook and the Radbournes!'

His tone changed slightly. 'If it were true then I would become the happiest man in the world. I love you, Vicky!'

She looked into his eyes, aware that this moment would never fade from her memory, and he kissed her and held her close while she confessed her love for him . . .

Twelfth Night finally arrived and Victoria sat in her room after tea, preparing for the last party of the season. She had saved her finest dress for this crowning event; of velvet in a golden shade, with a tight, low-cut bodice and wide sleeves that were slashed to show satin beneath. The skirt contained many yards of material. It was most becoming and she was aware of the fact, for it transformed her from a very attractive girl into a glowing beauty. Her dark eyes seemed wider and more appealing, her face greatly animated as she gazed at her reflection in the mirror. It was a miracle that a mere dress could effect such a transformation, and she dearly hoped that Thomas would find her presentable.

As she descended the staircase the hall reminded her of Christmas Eve, and for a moment she was gripped by a strange wistfulness. This was the end of the holiday and the days had fled all the faster because of the great pleasure they had contained. Yet she had known from the very beginning that reality could never be shrugged off, and it was here now, at her shoulder, awaiting the passing of time — the few remaining hours — before all this grandeur and delight were swept away into memory.

She paused suddenly, for Thomas was standing in the hall and Benjamin was with him. Thomas's guests had not yet started arriving. A pang stabbed through Victoria and she hurried to Thomas's side.

'What's wrong?' she demanded fearfully.

'It's Grandfather,' Benjamin said harshly. 'He's dying!'

The butler had already collected Victoria's bonnet and cloak and she donned them hurriedly, her face expressing concern.

'I'll go with you,' Thomas said instantly, but Victoria placed a hand upon his arm.

'No. You have your guests arriving shortly. I will go alone, and I'll keep you informed of developments.'

'I'll come over to Seabrook the moment the guests have gone,' Thomas promised as he glanced at the waiting Benjamin.

'It might be a long job,' Benjamin said, turning to the door. 'We'd best be on our way.' He opened the door and stalked off into the night, allowing a blast of icy air and a flurry of snow to sweep into the hall.

Victoria looked into Thomas's face. 'Please don't come over to Seabrook,' she begged. 'You know how badly Ashley behaves. I'll send word to you.'

He nodded silently, embraced her quickly and kissed her forehead. She sighed and departed, walking out into the driving snow, the freezing wind, and leaving behind the warmth and comfort of a holiday that was also in its death throes.

9

When they reached Seabrook, Seldon opened the door and Victoria immediately asked about her grandfather. The butler shook his head.

'Still the same, Miss. I fear he will be gone by morning.'

Victoria shivered, for the mansion was cold. Most of the lamps in the big chandelier had been extinguished and gloom adhered to the corners of the lofty hall. The blasting wind rattled the windows and shook the door. Benjamin went into the library and, as Victoria divested herself of her outer garments, Landers appeared in the library doorway.

'I'm sorry you had to be dragged away from your merry-making,' he said harshly. 'But you wished to be informed of your grandfather's end. The doctor feels that he will not see morning.'

'May I see him?'

'If he recovers consciousness.' Landers went back into the library, and Victoria saw Ashley standing inside the room, a wine glass in one hand.

She went to the stairs because she needed to change her dress. The gallery was deeply shadowed, and Victoria felt nervous as she went to her room. There was a lamp in the passage to the left, where Fenton's room was situated, but it gave off little more than a glow. She went to her room, changed, and, as she turned to leave, the door was opened and Marina confronted her.

'So you're back!'

'Naturally. I was sent for.' Victoria saw a spiteful expression upon Marina's face and compressed her lips. She was not in the mood for the hatred of her only kin. 'Is it of special interest to you?'

'I suppose you've been making up to Thomas.'

'I noticed that you were not present at any of the parties I attended.'

'Folk around here don't like the Radbournes, and we've never had any time for them. But Thomas is mine. You'll never get him.'

Victoria smiled. 'I have no intention of becoming involved in an argument with you, Marina,' she said. 'Perhaps you'll go.'

'You have a lot to learn about us,' Marina retorted, her dark eyes glittering. 'My father is living in the past, but Ashley and I have different ideas. We are no longer children, as Father will discover before he is very much older.'

Victoria suppressed a shudder as she recognised a threat in the malicious voice. Marina glared at her for a moment, then whirled away and flounced out of the doorway. For a moment Victoria stood thoughtful. Then she pulled herself free from her fears and went to the stairs. As she descended, Ashley emerged from the library, and she almost tripped in her haste to get clear before he could reach her. She heard his low, growling chuckle at her back, and when she entered the drawing room she was trembling.

Minutes later, Seldon appeared. He paced the length of the room and halted before her. Victoria regarded him expectantly. His face was ruddy in the firelight.

'Your Grandfather is conscious now and asking to see you,' he said.

Victoria started to her feet nervously. Seldon turned and walked back to the door and she followed him closely. He led the way up the staircase. She saw Landers and Ashley standing in the library doorway, watching her impassively, but she ignored them.

She was shown into Fenton's bedroom. The nurse was standing in the background, and a short, thickset man in a dark suit was at the bedside. Victoria went forward, suddenly apprehensive in the presence of encroaching death.

The doctor turned and glanced at her as the nurse came forward to turn up the wick of the lamp, chasing the shadows from the room and revealing

Fenton's waxen face. The sound of the old man's stertorous breathing rasped in the lofty room.

'You may stay only for a moment,' the doctor said. 'He's going, but he wants to see you.'

There was a silent protest in Victoria's mind, for Landers was down in the hall and he was Fenton's son. He had a right to spend the last minutes with his father. But she had not had the opportunity to see or talk to Fenton since that first day, and even as she bent over the old man she wondered if Landers had deliberately kept them apart.

'Fenton.' Doctor Royden's voice was incisive, and Fenton's eyelids flickered. 'Your granddaughter is here.'

Fenton's eyes flickered open. For a moment his gaze was unfocused. He was breathing harshly through his mouth. His features were stiff. Then animation filled his dark eyes and he peered up at Victoria. His lips moved several times before sound issued from them, and then his voice came, reedy and faint.

'Victoria! Durwood's daughter. I'm so happy you arrived in time for me to see you. If there is a here-after I shall soon be with your father again. I am weary of this world. It has been so lonely. But you are young and will make much of your life.'

'Don't tire yourself, Grandfather,' she pleaded.

'It does not matter now.' He was breathing shallowly, and she saw that his eyes were beginning to lose their brightness.

A faint sigh escaped him as he relaxed in death. Victoria gazed upon his immobile features for long moments, then drew a bitter sigh.

'May God have mercy upon his soul!' she whispered.

As the doctor led her from the room, tears stung Victoria's eyes but she blinked them away. She had witnessed death before. First her mother, then her father had died. But always there was pain from witnessing the passing of a soul, and she could only think of what her father and grandfather had missed in life. She hoped they could be together now.

Fenton's funeral was a quiet affair, and swiftly carried out. The estate workers stood in a little knot in the background as the stark coffin was carried out of the church by four men who slithered on the treacherous snow. The gate in the low fence around the family vault was standing wide and the heavy oak door that led down into the frozen ground was open.

Landers and his family were in pairs behind the coffin, and Victoria walked behind them. She noticed that Thomas and Amena were standing to the left of the gate, and for a moment her gaze rested upon Thomas's sad face. He nodded slightly and she acknowledged with a slight movement of her head.

The vault was cold and dank. A score of coffins rested in two orderly rows along either side of its length. The pall-bearers deposited their burden in its place and then departed, and the village priest completed the funeral service that had begun in the church. Landers moved to the steps leading out almost before the last echo of the priest's voice had faded, but Victoria remained beside the coffin, her thoughts troubled.

When they went out into the foreboding daylight the torches were extinguished and the heavy door of the vault slammed with a dull sound that echoed in Victoria's heart. The priest led her to a waiting carriage and she entered thankfully. She saw Thomas again and lifted a hand to him.

The funeral party returned to Seabrook. Rain was turning the snow to slush and the sky was grey, filled with billowing clouds that sailed burdensomely overhead. Victoria saw that the curtains had been opened during their absence, and Seldon was standing at the door, his face expressing relief, but he betrayed no emotion as Landers stalked past him, followed closely by Ashley, Marina and Benjamin. Victoria walked into the hall, shivering violently, and a maid took her outer garments. Seldon closed the front door with a slam that echoed through the house.

'Mr Spilsby is waiting in the library,' he announced.

Ashley glared at Victoria as they followed Landers across the hall. Victoria steeled herself for what would be an ordeal, but she spared a thought for the poor, frail body that was now at eternal rest amongst the mouldering bones of its ancestors.

When they entered the library she saw that the lawyer was standing before the big fire, and Landers was already seated in an easy chair, oblivious to the niceties of etiquette. Marina was also seated, but Ashley and Benjamin were standing behind Landers' chair. Spilsby came to lead Victoria to the left, where she sat just outside the half circle formed by Landers and Marina and slightly to the rear, where she would not be forced to meet their concerted gaze. A tense silence fell upon the room as Spilsby waited until Seldon had ushered in all the servants, who huddled together in the background.

'I shall now read the last will and testament of the recently departed master of Seabrook,' Spilsby said, unfolding the document. His tone was crisp, as if he were in a court of law and the will was an indictment. He cleared his throat and began, 'I Fenton, Stanford, Radbourne of Seabrook Manor, Cornwall, hereby revoke all former wills and codicils and declare this to be my last will and testament. I appoint Millard Spilsby of Tregston, Cornwall, and his son Woodward Spilsby, solicitor of Tregston, Cornwall, to be my executors.'

Spilsby paused and glanced around, his watery eyes glinting. The tension seemed to catch at Victoria's throat and she drew a shuddering breath. Landers crossed his legs and leaned back in his seat, his hands gripping the arms of the chair.

'Get on with it and stop doddering,' he snapped.

'To Landers my son,' Spilsby continued drily, 'who caused me so much loneliness and heartache I leave Thornton Grange as his home for the rest of his life and the revenue from that part of the Seabrook estate which is connected to the grange as his living. The children of Landers named Ashley and Marina and Benjaman shall have the right to live at Thornton Grange for the rest of their lives but none of the children of the said Ashley and Marina and Benjamin shall inherit Thornton Grange which shall return to the owner of Seabrook Manor when Landers and his children are dead. I bequeath nothing to Ashley and Marina and Benjamin as I expect Landers to provide for them from the revenue of Thornton Grange.'

A ripple flitted through the lofty room, and Spilsby again glanced around at the intent faces peering at him. He alone knew the full details of the will, and he was unemotional as he returned his attention to the document that quivered slightly in his shaking hands and continued to read.

'I give and bequeath the sum of one hundred pounds free of all duties to my butler Seldon for good and loyal service and one hundred pounds free of all duties to my housekeeper Miss Maitland for her perseverance and spiritual guidance through the bitterness of my life. I give and bequeath to all household servants in my employ at the time of my death each the sum of ten pounds free of all duties and charge them to serve my heir with loyalty.'

'I've heard enough!' Landers interrupted, springing to his feet.

'Sir,' Spilsby reproved firmly, 'please allow me to continue.'

'There's nothing here for me and my brood, and I have no wish to listen to the disposal of my home to a foreign stranger!' Landers turned, motioning for his family to accompany him, and strode to the door, followed by Ashley,

Marina and Benjamin. They looked neither left nor right, and Victoria clenched her hands as she watched them. The door slammed behind them, and only then did tension filter out of the atmosphere.

Spilsby's face showed anger, and he compressed his bloodless lips before continuing.

'I give and bequeath all the residue of my property real and personal to my granddaughter Victoria Radbourne. In the event of the death without issue of Victoria Radbourne the estate will pass into the hands of Landers Radbourne, upon whose death Ashley Radbourne will inherit.' Spilsby looked up with a sigh. 'The will is signed by Fenton and witnessed by two clerks in the office of my son's practice in Tregston. Let me be the first to congratulate you, Victoria. And I must say that I am very happy indeed to have been instrumental in discovering your existence and locating you in time for Fenton to meet you. He died happy, I think, and perhaps your arrival had made up in part for the bitter years he suffered.'

'Thank you!' Victoria went forward and shook hands with the lawyer. 'You have my eternal thanks, sir! Now my father may rest easy in his grave. Justice has been done.'

Seldon came towards them carrying a tray with a decanter and glasses upon it. The servants had departed, and the butler smiled as he poured wine.

'May I congratulate you, Mistress Victoria? This is a momentous day for me.'

'We all seem to be elated with the exception of Landers and his family.' There was no joy in Victoria's tone.

'Spare them no pity,' Spilsby said. 'If you feel charitable towards them then remember your father and his circumstances. He might still be alive if it were not for Landers.'

In the ensuing silence Spilsby toasted Victoria, then set down his glass. 'Now, my dear young lady, I have discharged the last of my duties to Fenton

Radbourne. I have seen you installed as the Mistress of Seabrook Manor. In future your business will be in the hands of my son, and I have already instructed him in the matter of watching over your interests.'

'Thank you. I'll see you to the door.' Victoria shook the old lawyer's hand once more. She followed as Seldon led the way into the hall, and after the lawyer's departure she asked Seldon to return to the library with her.

Seldon ushered her back to a comfortable seat by the blazing fire and then stood attendance upon her.

'I know that you and Miss Maitland are to be trusted implicitly,' she said thoughtfully. 'You are also more familiar with the characters of Landers' branch of the family, and I leave you in no doubt that I suspect they have taken this development of my inheritance very badly indeed. I don't know when Landers will move to Thornton Grange, but I do ask you to remain alert for any kind of trouble that might arise between now and the time they depart.'

'I have been on guard from the moment you first stepped across the threshold, Miss Victoria. I must admit that I am concerned for your safety.'

'Thank you.' Victoria tried to fight down her bleak thoughts. 'I promise that you will see a great many changes around here.'

'And all for the better, I am sure.' Seldon picked up the tray and departed, with Victoria following him into the hall.

Victoria dreaded the thought of lunch, but later, when she entered the dining room, it was deserted, and Seldon arrived to inform her that Landers had taken his entire family into Tregston.

That afternoon, Thomas and Amena arrived, and Thomas came immediately to confront Victoria, hand outstretched, offering his congratulations. Amena hugged her, and Seabrook seemed to gain in atmosphere, or so it seemed to Victoria as she led the way into the drawing room. Now that Landers and his family were out of the house and she could imagine Seabrook becoming exactly like Briarwood.

'I wish I could have stood at your side this morning,' Thomas said, holding Victoria's hands as they warmed themselves before the great fire. 'I have missed you, Victoria. My thoughts are constantly with you. It has been brought home to me just how much I have come to love you.'

Amena had moved out of earshot to the window, and Victoria glanced towards the girl as she replied softly.

'I love you, too, Thomas, more than I can possibly say.'

'I'd be happier about all of this if you would come to stay at Briarwood until Landers and his family have moved out,' he urged.

'I'd like nothing better than to accept your offer, but I am now the mistress here and I'm anxious to get this place into shape so that I can ask you and Amena here. There are a great many things to be done. Landers has not been industrious in keeping the house in good repair.'

Thomas nodded. 'If I can be of help in any way then don't hesitate to let me know,' he said firmly.

'As a matter of fact I'd like to talk to you about a number of things,' Victoria continued. 'I shall have to go into Tregston to see the lawyer about the estate. Then I'll need to learn how to manage a place like this.'

'I'll give you some lessons,' Thomas offered.

Victoria sighed. 'Well,' she said in a relieved tone. 'It has come to pass. My sacred vow is accomplished.'

'Perhaps now you will be able to devote some time to your own life,' Thomas observed. He took her into his arms and kissed her gently, and all Victoria's cares fled under the pressure of the new emotions that filled her mind.

There was a discreet knock at the door and Seldon entered. 'Your pardon, Miss Victoria,' he said. 'The Radbourne carriage is approaching. There's a great deal of snow falling. It could be a blizzard coming. Master Thomas, you might be well advised to start back to Briarwood. I fear that the roads will be well nigh impassable shortly.'

'Thank you, Seldon.' Victoria glanced at Thomas as the butler withdrew. She sighed. 'I hope that Landers and Ashley have not been drinking.'

'I'll remain if you wish,' he replied firmly. 'I certainly don't want to leave you alone at their mercy. The situation has changed now, remember. You are the mistress of Seabrook. The business has been settled.'

'Thank you. But Ashley is always violently angered by the sight of you. And Marina is jealous of the fact that we have become friends. She suspects, too, that we have become more than that to each other.'

'Although she is female, Marina is cast in the same harsh mould as the rest of her family.' Thomas was tight-lipped. 'For as long as I can remember I have striven to discourage her. But I suspect that Landers has had something to do with her attitude. He would have Briarwood under his control as well as Seabrook.'

'Did Marina ever have an understanding with you?' Victoria asked.

'Did she tell you that?' He chuckled in a harsh tone. 'She would like to think there had been, but I never could stand the sight of her, as Amena will vouch. But with a woman like Marina it is almost impossible to remain remote. She has acted shamelessly in trying to attract my interest.'

Victoria nodded, relieved by his words. Marina's attempts to prevent the growth of a natural friendship arising between Thomas and herself had failed completely, as her father had failed in his long endeavours to secure Seabrook.

10

Landers came into the house, followed by Ashley, Marina and Benjamin, as Thomas and Amena were in the hall preparing to leave. Seldon was helping Amena into her cloak when the front door burst open, and snow came flurrying over the threshold, chivvied by the merciless wind, until the butler hurried to close the door. Victoria shook hands with Amena, and Thomas clasped Victoria's hand at the moment of parting, unmindful of the fact that Landers and his brood stared while divesting themselves of their outer garments.

'I'll come and see you tomorrow morning,' Thomas said softly, and Victoria felt like telling him to wait for her. But she fought down the impulse and turned to go up to her room.

Neither Landers nor any of his three

offspring spoke to Victoria, or, indeed, took any notice of her as she started ascending the stairs. The silence that filled the hall was hostile, and Victoria felt icy shivers darting along her spine. She heard Ashley's voice but failed to make out what he said. Landers spoke sharply.

'You will not, Ashley!' His tone was such that Victoria glanced down the stairs to see Ashley on the bottom stair and look as if he were ascending after her. 'Come into the library, all of you,' Landers continued, sharply. 'I want to talk to you. That includes you, Benjamin.'

Victoria continued up to the gallery, hands clenched. She heard muttered protests from Ashley and Benjamin, but when she glanced down at the hall, Landers was ushering his family into the library. She drew a deep breath, held it for a moment, then exhaled slowly. Acting upon an impulse, she went along to Landers' room and entered. She lifted the floorboard by the fireplace, kneeled and peered through the peep-hole, heart pounding madly and hands trembling.

She saw Landers standing with his back to the blazing fire. Marina had seated herself in one of the armchairs and Benjamin was lounging on the couch. Moving slightly, Victoria saw Ashley helping himself to a drink. Landers' harsh voice floated easily to the ceiling.

'I won't tell any of you again that this business will be handled my way. I've waited too long to get my hands on this estate. I started all of this years before any of you were born. All the stories you heard about me usurping my brother Durwood were true. I would have killed him in cold blood if he hadn't been exiled. That's how determined I am to win. So I won't tolerate any of your interference.'

'We've been waiting and waiting,' Ashley rasped, 'and nothing has been done. Victoria has been here more than a month now and still you wait.'

'I couldn't do anything until Fenton's will was read,' Landers retorted. 'There was still a chance that I might have inherited, and if so then further action would not have been necessary.'

'Well, now you know you haven't inherited,' Marina cut in. 'So what are you going to do? You can't have another murder in the house so soon.'

'Murder?' Ashley rounded on his sister. 'I told you what happened to Elizabeth.' He glowered angrily. 'She fell!'

'I saw what happened,' Benjamin interrupted. 'I was prowling around in the dark like I always do. That night I rattled Victoria's door a couple of times to scare her if she was awake, and then I heard Elizabeth blundering around, probably looking for another drink. I was going to put her back to bed when you came out of your room, Ashley. I saw you push her down the stairs.'

Victoria turned cold with horror as she listened. They were discussing murder as if it were a normal activity!

But what about herself? She pressed closer to the peep-hole, hoping to learn more.

'Shut up, all of you,' Landers snapped. 'The way Elizabeth was going around, it would have been only a matter of time before she fell. Ashley merely hurried things up. It's about time he did something right. The way he tried to drop that beam on Victoria in the old mansion was nothing short of rank stupidity. It might have scared her away completely so that we couldn't get at her.'

Benjamin laughed mockingly and Landers turned on him.

'Do you think you were clever, locking her in the attic and trying to scare her? Ha! She'd take a lot of scaring. I admire her nerve, and could wish that she was my daughter if she didn't stand between me and Seabrook.'

'I took that opportunity when I saw where she was going,' Benjamin protested angrily, getting to his feet. 'If that's all the thanks I get then you can do this without my help. I'm sick of the whole business.'

He moved towards the door and Victoria replaced the floorboard and hurriedly left the room. She could hear Benjamin ascending the stairs as she went into her own room, and her hands were trembling as she bolted herself in.

She wished she could have heard more, but what she had learned made her senses whirl with horror. Now what was she to do? The question was instinctive, and the obvious answer came readily to mind. She had to get to Thomas immediately!

Crossing to the window, she peered out into the darkness to see that a blizzard was raging as Seldon had forecast. But she would rather risk losing herself out there than stay another night at the Manor. All she needed were her cloak and bonnet, and an opportunity to sneak from the house unobserved. Somehow she would traverse those six treacherous miles to Briarwood.

A noise at the door alerted her and she hurried to it, standing breathless, straining her ears for the slightest unnatural sound. She heard a scraping noise outside, and then saw the door handle move slightly. She gulped, terribly afraid. They were coming for her!

But nothing happened and she stood in the heavy silence, hardly daring to breathe. Her heart was pounding powerfully, shaking her with its insistence, and she slowly realised that she was too afraid to attempt to get away. If she tried and they caught her she would have no hope. But if she remained bolted in the room then she ought to be safe until morning. With servants in the house, Landers would not dare attempt anything openly.

Going to the bed, she made herself comfortable and read a little to pass the time, being relieved when it was finally late enough for her to retire. Fierce gusts of wind were rattling the window as she snuggled under the covers and tried to relax. She dozed intermittently, vowing that as soon as morning came she would flee to Briarwood and Thomas. But she was unable to rest completely because of the fears and stress in her mind, although she fell asleep finally, worn out both physically and mentally.

Then suddenly she was wide awake, heart pounding. Raising her head from the pillow, she saw that the fire had burned itself out and realised that a considerable time had elapsed since she retired. She listened intently, wondering if she had dreamed the disturbance, and heard a sharp, metallic sound that brought her fears quickly into focus.

The sound came from the window. She sat up instantly, fully alert, aware that it could not have been made naturally. She gulped. There it was again! It sounded just like a giant rat gnawing at the woodwork, but with a metallic quality.

She slid out of bed and began to dress, her fingers trembling. The sounds were continuing, and she was aware that someone was trying to break into the room. She drew a quivering breath, wondering if this were a part of some monstrous nightmare. The noise at the window was becoming more persistent, and she stood in the centre of the room gazing at the drawn curtains, imagining all kinds of nameless horrors out there in the night trying to get in at her.

Plucking up her courage, she went to the curtains and dragged them open. The exterior window ledge was about three feet wide, and there was a dark figure crouched upon it, outlined against the gleaming snow. The noises which had disturbed her were being made by a long-bladed knife that was being forced in against the window catch.

Victoria almost fainted in shock. Fear seemed to freeze her blood. The light reflecting from the snow revealed details of the dark figure and she recognised Ashley. The nameless dread left her with that realisation but her fear was undiminished, for Ashley paused in his efforts to force the window and waved the knife threateningly at her before resuming his attack.

Panic swept through Victoria as she drew the curtains to blot out the frightening scene. She ran to the door and unlocked it, but when she tried to open it, the door refused to budge. She turned the key back and forth several times, thinking that the old lock had jammed, but heard the tumblers working normally and finally came to the conclusion that the door was fastened on the outside. She had locked herself in to prevent unwanted entry, but someone had fastened it to prevent her leaving.

She had the presence of mind to relock the door before turning away from it, and now was shivering with panic. But desperation drove away her fear, pushing it into the back of her mind. The terrible sounds of Ashley trying to force the window never ceased, and she realised that it could only be a matter of time before he succeeded in opening it. She hurried back to the window and dragged aside the curtains once more, revealing the ominous figure squatting on the sill.

Horror filled her when she saw that the point of the knife blade was between the edges of the window and pressing against the catch. Even as she watched, the catch began to slip downward under the pressure being applied, and she froze in shock. Ashley was succeeding. He was opening the window! There was a sharp crack as the catch slipped free.

Ashley's face was obscured by shadows, but his teeth gleamed in the faint light as he began to ease backwards on the slippery sill in order to drag open the window. Victoria was transfixed by horror, but his movement broke her paralysis and she moved instinctively, without conscious thought. Stepping forward, she lifted her hands and thrust against the window with all her desperate strength. The window flew open, catching Ashley off guard, and he lost his balance on the snow-covered sill and uttered a fearful shriek as he was hurled backwards into dark space.

Victoria gasped for breath, almost blundering through the open window as she was carried forward by the momentum of her violent action. Her hands skidded on the sill and she came to rest with her head and shoulders out of the window, her face towards the stone terrace three storeys below. Ashley's crumpled body lay motionless down there, and she drew back in horror, hastily closing the window and forcing down the handle to tighten the catch. She felt her legs crumpling in shock and staggered to the bed, sinking upon it in a fit of violent trembling.

What was happening? The question burned in her mind. And why was her door fastened on the outside? She forced herself up from the bed and staggered to the door, unlocking it again and trying to open it. But it would not budge and she relocked it, ensuring that it was locked on her side before returning to the window.

Trembling with apprehension, she peered out, half afraid that hands would snatch at her, but there was no sign of danger, and when she looked down at the terrace Ashley still lay motionless.

She realised that Ashley had used the thick creeper on the wall to climb up to her window. Forcing herself to be resolute, she clambered upon the sill and eased herself out through the window. There were only a few flakes of snow falling now and the night was surprisingly clear although heavy clouds obscured the stars. But the snow itself added lightness to the shadows, and she closed her eyes as she slipped on the sill and almost made a fatal plunge from her hazardous perch. Moving carefully, grasping the sill with deathly grip, she swung her legs out and down to the creeper, finding a perilous foothold. Then she eased backwards, reaching with her right hand until she grasped a snow covered branch. The night air was freezing and the wind buffeted her as if delighting in the opportunity to wrench her chilled fingers from their precarious hold.

She began to edge sideways, making for the window on her left, and within moments she was almost frozen. Her teeth chattered and her fingers lost all feeling. Twice her feet slipped from the creeper and her whole weight came to rest upon her slender arms. She closed her eyes and prayed, reaching blindly for fresh footholds and continuing. After what seemed an eternity she was directly beneath the window and, as she reached up with stiff fingers to try and open it, she was horrified to see a ruddy glow emanating from the storey below, exactly beneath her room.

She reached out with hands that were so frozen that all feeling in them was absent. But she found the window unlocked and tried to drag it open. Her hands were strengthless, seemed not to belong to her, and she could not force her fingers to take hold. Weakness suddenly welled up from inside, and for many dreadful moments she fancied that she would lose her hold and plunge down to join the motionless Ashley on the terrace.

But thoughts of her father, and of Thomas, strengthened her resolve and she dragged the window open. At first her attempts to get over the sill were unsuccessful, but she clenched her teeth and willed herself to move. She was panting as she finally slid across the sill to fall into a crumpled heap upon the floor.

But fear drove her on. That red glow could only mean that the mansion was on fire! She pushed herself upright on trembling legs and paused only to snatch a poker from the fireplace. Then she hurried to the door, which stood open, and peered out into the gloomy passage.

Her first action was to go to her own door, and she soon discovered why she had been unable to open it from the inside. A metal hook had been screwed into the doorpost and the handle was tied to it. She moved back along the passage to the stairs, shocked by the frightening developments, and halted breathlessly when she found her way barred by a raging inferno of leaping flames.

Smoke was billowing up the stairs, choking her, causing her eyes to stream, and she turned quickly, aware that there was a second flight of stairs at the rear of the house which was used by the servants. She hurriedly passed her room and followed the passage towards the rear of the wing. Darkness shrouded her and she gripped the poker tightly, ready to fight for her life against anyone who accosted her.

Relief struggled through the horror in her mind when she discovered the narrow back stairs and began to descend. She reached a landing and paused, for the glow of the fire was showing lower down, and above the fearsome sound of crackling wood she heard voices arguing stridently. One was Marina's voice, she recognised, and the other belonged to a man. She shrank back into the deeper shadows of the landing when two figures appeared and began to ascend the stairs facing her. The growing red glow at their backs prevented her from seeing their faces, but the man was leading and the woman was a stair or two lower down.

When the man had almost reached the landing Victoria stepped forward, swinging the poker, and delivered a furious blow to his head. He caught her movement from the shadows at the last moment and flung up his arm to ward off the blow. But Victoria heard the sickening thud of metal connecting with his skull. He uttered a choking cry and pitched over backwards, plunging down the stairs and crashing into Marina, who uttered a high-pitched scream. Both figures went tumbling down to the lower landing and Victoria hurried after them, afraid that they would rise to attack her. She fancied the man was Benjamin . . .

The figures lay motionless, and Victoria approached them cautiously. Marina was lying partially beneath the man, having broken his fall. The seat of the fire was on this lower floor and its ruddy glow was bright and menacing. Victoria gasped in shock as she bent over the men, for it wasn't Benjamin, or even Landers. It was Thomas!

She sank to the floor at his side, staring uncomprehendingly at his pale features. His face was upturned. There was a dark smear of blood on his forehead and she touched it gingerly, discovering a large bruise where the poker had struck him. He seemed to be deeply unconscious, and she feared that she had killed him. Her fingers trembled as she felt for a heartbeat, and almost cried out in relief when she found it thumping strongly. She dropped the poker and grasped his shoulders, pulling him away from Marina.

Turning her attention to the girl,

Victoria cried out in horror, for even in the garish half-light she could see that Marina's head was lying at an unnatural angle to her shoulders. The terrible truth struck her. Marina's neck was broken! She had cushioned Thomas's fall and was dead!

Victoria sobbed as she grasped Thomas under the arms and tried to drag him down the next flight of stairs. Smoke was thickening with each passing moment, and the fearsome roaring of the conflagration increased as the hungry flames devoured the old woodwork of the house. But Thomas was too heavy for her to manage, and she was afraid that he might slip from her grasp and plunge down yet another flight of stairs. She straightened, aware that she desperately needed help. Seldon would do. Anyone but Landers or Benjamin. Her mind reeled under the stresses of the nightmarish situation.

She turned around to seek help, and then screamed, for Landers was standing close behind her, his features twisted with hatred, eyes glaring in the flickering light coming from the raging fire.

Victoria hurled herself to where she had dropped the poker but Landers approached and kicked it aside. Then he grasped her with big, cruel hands, hurting her shoulders. She struggled ineffectually to get free.

'You fiend!' she gasped. 'What do you hope to achieve by this? Already your scheming has killed Ashley and Marina.'

'And Marina?' he demanded. His lips compressed when he saw his daughter lying dead upon the floor. 'So! You would cheat me of my triumph! Well, there is an end to it. There must be no marks of violence upon you.' His voice rasped heavily. 'But there won't be anything left of you by the time the fire burns itself out. Come along. It's no use struggling. You can't get away from me. I'm not going to make any mistake. I have Ashley to thank for all this trouble. He wanted to get his hands on you. I told him that one day his lusts would be the death of him and the fool has borne out my prediction.'

'You feel no grief for Ashley or Marina,' Victoria accused. 'What kind of man are you?'

Landers made no reply. He dragged Victoria back up the stairs, cursing when she tried to delay him. But there was little she could do. He was powerfully built, and used his strength cruelly, dragging her effortlessly up the stairs to the passage where her bedroom was situated, above the heart of the fire on the lower floor.

The handle of her door was still tied to the hook that had been screwed into the doorpost and Landers tried to hold her with one hand while he untied the cord with the other. She struggled to break free and he paused in his efforts to cuff her.

'Stand still,' he commanded.

Victoria caught a glimpse of movement in the smoky atmosphere behind Landers and gasped in horror. Landers turned his head quickly, alerted by her movement. Benjamin was approaching, walking slowly. His jacket was smouldering, his face blackened. His hair was singed and his eyes were wide, filled with unreasoning rage.

'Who started the fire?' he demanded.

'I did!' Landers tightened his grip upon Victoria as she tried again to break away. 'This is only the old wing. It won't matter if it burns down. But I'd raze the whole estate to the ground rather than permit it to fall into the hands of anyone but me.'

'I've worked this estate for years,' Benjamin snapped. 'But you and Ashley have done nothing. Now you burn the place!' He uttered a snarling growl of rage and struck Landers a terrific blow in the face. Landers lost his hold upon Victoria and fell against the wall, then straightened with an oath and hurled himself at his youngest son. But Benjamin struck him again. 'I saw Ashley dead on the terrace,' he snarled. 'It's all your doing. The thought of owning Seabrook has turned your mind. You've been crazy for years. You're even prepared to burn the place to the ground rather than see someone else get it. Well, if you want Seabrook you can have it.'

Victoria cowered against the door, hands clasped at her breast. Thick smoke was swirling along the passage, making her eyes water, and she began to cough unrestrainedly as it clogged her lungs. She saw Benjamin seize hold of his father and attempt to lift him bodily. Landers struck at him, using fearsome strength, but Benjamin, carrying his father, turned and walked back along the passage the way he had come, towards the top of the main stairs where the fire was fiercest. It suddenly dawned upon Victoria what was in Benjamin's mind and she stifled a scream. Landers was unable to break his son's hold, and was carried along as if he were a child.

Flames were shooting up the main stairs and they cast the figures of Landers and Benjamin in a grotesque silhouette. Benjamin was dragging his father towards the inferno, shouting at the top of his voice as he did so. Landers was calling out urgently, but to no avail. They became indistinct in the swirling smoke as Victoria watched. Then there was an ominous rumbling sound and the floor where they were standing collapsed in a fiery shower of flames and sparks. Smoke billowed up and heat seared along the passage. Landers and Benjamin vanished instantly, still locked together.

Victoria closed her eyes for a moment, but fear moved her and she hurried back the way Landers had brought her. When she reached the landing where Marina lay the flames were almost licking around the girl's body. Victoria hurried to where Thomas was weakly attempting to get to his hands and knees and helped him up. The heat was overpowering. Flames were roaring along the passage and flaring up the walls to lick voraciously at the ceiling. She cringed from the inferno as they staggered to the back stairs and continued their descent. Thomas was groaning, his senses bewildered, and Victoria clung to him, uttering words of encouragement as they passed through the nightmare.

When they reached the ground floor there was an open door which gave access to the snow covered terrace. As they passed out into the freezing night Victoria gave thanks to God in a breathless voice. A shadow moved and then a figure materialised. It was Seldon. He came hurrying to their side when he saw them, helping them out into the cold night air, where they paused and breathed deeply. The first thing that Victoria saw when she was able to look around was Ashley's inert body stretched out upon the snow, and a shudder passed through her.

'Master Landers ordered everyone out of the house when the fire was discovered,' Seldon said anxiously. 'He wouldn't let anyone else take the risk of trying to fetch you to safety. He insisted upon going himself.'

Victoria took great gulps of the freezing air and helped Thomas farther away from the building. A menacing red glare filled the night, making the snow look as if it were stained with blood. Thomas straightened, recovering quickly in the fresh air. He placed a hand under Victoria's elbow and they stumbled through the snow to the shelter of the opposite wing. Other figures were moving in the surrounding night, and Victoria realised that they were the estate workers come to help fight the fire.

'I don't know what happened,' Thomas said in a wondering tone. 'I was ascending the stairs when it seemed that the roof fell in upon me.'

Victoria drew a shuddering breath. Explanations could wait, but there was one thing she wanted to know.

'How did you come to be in the house with Marina?' she asked.

They entered the opposite wing and crossed the library.

'I was trying to keep an eye on you,' Thomas confessed. 'I saw flames when I was in the grounds. I've been sneaking around outside every night for a long time now, just watching and checking. I broke in, and Marina saw me. She was trying to stop me getting to your room.'

'I know the rest,' Victoria cut in, sighing heavily. She was weak and shaken, trembling with reaction, but the course of events had been too horrific for her mind to fully absorb, and shock partially blotted out the grim reality of what had happened.

Seldon appeared in the doorway, dishevelled and breathless, and he nodded at the sight of their strained faces.

'I think the fire will be contained in the old wing,' he reported. 'The estate workers have got water pouring into the blaze. Seabrook won't burn down.'

'Thank you, Seldon.' Victoria closed her eyes for an instant, fighting against fatigue and reaction. Then she looked at Thomas, saw the great bruise upon his forehead, and relief swept through her. She called to Seldon as the butler turned to leave. 'Has Landers come out of the old wing?' she asked, although she was aware that he was dead.

'No, Miss.' The old butler shook his head. 'And no-one can get in there at the moment.' For a moment he paused and studied her face, his doubts plain upon his features. She guessed that he was thinking that the fire could not be accidental, that perhaps Landers himself had set it deliberately. But she did not want that story to get out. 'Landers showed us the way out through the smoke and then went back to look for Benjamin,' she said.

Thomas opened his eyes and stared at her, caught her expression, and nodded slowly.

'Yes,' he said.

'We have Landers to thank for our lives. Be sure to remember that, Seldon, when the questions are asked about this night.'

The butler nodded, staring first at

Victoria, then at Thomas. Victoria thought of her father, and Fenton, recently buried, and knew that it could be no other way. As Seldon departed she heaved a sigh. The situation was grim but the nightmare was over. She was now the mistress of Seabrook. Durwood's birthright had passed to her, and final justice for the cruel scheme that had ruined the happiness of two generations of Radbournes had finally been wrought by the fire. But, more than that, she could tell by the expression on Thomas's pale face that one day she would become the mistress of Briarwood. Time was all-encompassing and would erase the sharpness of this horror. Then they would be at liberty to enjoy the future and all it promised.

We do hope that you have enjoyed reading this large print book.

Did you know that all of our titles are available for purchase?

We publish a wide range of high quality large print books including:
Romances, Mysteries, Classics
General Fiction
Non Fiction and Westerns

Special interest titles available in large print are:
The Little Oxford Dictionary
Music Book, Song Book
Hymn Book, Service Book

Also available from us courtesy of Oxford University Press:
Young Readers' Dictionary
(large print edition)
Young Readers' Thesaurus
(large print edition)

For further information or a free brochure, please contact us at:
Ulverscroft Large Print Books Ltd.,
The Green, Bradgate Road, Anstey,
Leicester, LE7 7FU, England.
Tel: (00 44) 0116 236 4325
Fax: (00 44) 0116 234 0205

SINISTER ISLE OF LOVE

Phyllis Mallett

Jenny Carr is joining her brother on the Caribbean island of Taminga to start a new life. On her way, she meets Peter Blaine, a successful businessman on the island. He couldn't be more of a contrast to Craig Hannant, whose business is failing. His wife had died in mysterious circumstances, and Craig is now a difficult man to be around — but Jenny falls for Craig, despite all the signs that she is making the biggest mistake of her life . . .

CUPID'S BOW

Toni Anders

When romantic novelist Janey first meets Ashe Corby, she is not impressed. But frustratingly, the hero in the latest novel she is writing persists in resembling him! As Janey gets to know Ashe, she comes to admire and like him. But when she attempts to help Ashe's son Daniel to realise his dream of studying horticulture, Ashe is furious at what he sees as interference on Janey's part. Miserable without each other, will love win through for them?

MISTLETOE MEDICINE

Anna Ramsay

Ever since he wrecked her romance with Dickie Derby, Nurse Hannah Westcott has harboured a thorough dislike of Dr Jonathan Boyd-Harrington — but she never expected to see him again. To her horror, he turns up as Senior Registrar at the Royal Hanoverian Hospital, and there is no way she can avoid him — especially when he takes an interest in the hospital panto. Hannah has the star part, but it would seem she must play Nurse Beauty to Jonathan Boyd-Harrington's Dr Beast . . .

LEAP YEAR

Marilyn Fountain

Tired of the city rush, Erin Mallowson takes a twelve-month lease on Owl Cottage in Norfolk to run her own image consultancy business. Her ex-boss and commitment-phobic boyfriend Spencer thinks she's mad. Keen to embrace the village lifestyle, Erin doesn't expect it to include the enigmatic Brad Cavill, a former footballer with a troubled past. But even though work and love refuse to run smoothly, it turns out to be a leap year that Erin never wants to end . . .